SEEDS OF TRUER NATURES

SEEDS OF TRUER NATURES

A PRIMA MATERIA NOVELLA

L.S. JOHNSON

TRAVERSING Z PRESS

Traversing Z Press, P.O. Box 990, San Leandro, CA 94577

www.traversingz.com

ISBN (paperback): 978-0-9988936-9-3

ISBN (ebook): 978-0-9988936-8-6

Library of Congress Control Number: 2021921884

Editing by Richard Shealy

Cover art by Welder Wings

Cover design by Najla Qamber

Interior design and project management by Jennifer Uhlich

Printed in the United States of America

CONTENTS

DRAMATIS PERSONAE

Adrian, an erin, created by Gabriel Berger
Fra Domenico, a Dominican monk
Fra Girolamo, a Dominican monk
Lorenzo di Piero de' Medici, a citizen of Florence, father of Piero
Magnus, an erin, created by Adrian
Niccolò Michelozzi, secretary to Lorenzo
Piero di Lorenzo de' Medici, a citizen of Florence, son of Lorenzo
Seissan, an erin, created by Gabriel Berger
Fra Tommaso, a Dominican monk
The *Skìa*, Gabriel Berger's chosen agents
A young Franciscan novice
A nattering merchant
Several horses who deserve heavenly rewards
A herd of pigs, who are also quite deserving

Several words in this story, such as erin, are in a language called
Sereidenikè. A glossary is available in the back of the book.

He that knoweth not what he seeketh, shall not know what he shall find.

    - *The Crowning of Nature*

Italy

The late fifteenth century

1

THE MONK COLLAPSED as night fell, tumbling into the brush at the side of the road, the snapping of branches like firecrackers; Magnus bit back his cry of triumph at the sight. Birds rose up at the crash, then settled again, and all was silent once more. Past the heap of the body was an expanse of wild fields, and beyond that, copses of browning trees spiked with green-black cypress, all the way to the horizon; but this was an illusion, for ahead the road rose slightly, and if one were to crest that next hill, they would come in sight of stone walls enclosing a hospice, promising food and shelter to all who made it to the gate.

The monk, of course, had not made it to the gate, and thus as matters stood he was fucked. Just as Magnus had predicted. In all likelihood, he had expected God to guide his steps to Florence, and God in His infinite wisdom had flicked the monk aside like so much refuse. Now he was little more than a heap of filthy fabrics, with two blistered feet sticking out, clad in leather that barely remembered being sandals.

"Well," said Adrian wearily, "that is a pathetic sight, and I have seen my share of pathetic sights."

Magnus looked down at his genetes's bowed, dark head and held out his hand. They had switched to Tuscan some weeks ago in preparation, until the lilting syllables came naturally once again; but certain words, like genetes, seemed to resist translation. What in Tuscan could encompass all that Adrian was to him, or what they were in themselves?

With a pained sigh, Adrian felt around in his satchel, then dropped a stack of coins into Magnus's upturned palm. "Unlike your gloating, which is merely sickening," he continued. "Now what do we do?"

"Drink him," Magnus opined, letting the tips of his fangs show as he counted the coins. "How far do you think we are from the hospice?"

"Another word out of your mouth and I will vomit, Magnus; I swear it."

"I believe I wagered not only that he would never make the hospice, he would drop less than a half day's walk from its door."

"I will vomit on your boots."

"With your ample wager, I can buy new ones." He shrugged at Adrian's exasperated groan. "I have no idea what you thought to accomplish with him, anyway. What does it matter that he's going the same way? We can be in Florence in a few nights if we move quickly. Let's just go and steal the damn book."

But Adrian was shaking his head. "How many times must I tell you? We cannot simply *steal* it. If we *steal* it, every sereides, every erin from Buda to the sea will know what we are about. We need to take it without upset. We need"—he pointed dramatically at the heap of fabric—"an *intercessor*."

"Adrian, there isn't a dangen for thirty days in any direction—"

"They *always* know, Magnus." Adrian spoke through gritted teeth. "A lesson I thought you had finally learned."

Magnus flushed and looked away, out at the last thin line of purple horizon, the fields dappled with shadows. He had not meant it like that; he had only meant to ease Adrian's fears. Of course he had learned; how could he not have learned? Their last time in Gotland was forever seared in his memory, and months later it still tainted their every action. They had been punished by their king before, but never before had Gabriel punished them for each other's actions. To know someone else was suffering *for* you, *because* of you … oh, it had shaken Magnus badly, but it had done something more to Adrian, something he didn't understand and Adrian wouldn't acknowledge. Even now, this stupid business with the book, it was all Gotland still, Gotland and Adrian's fear of what happened there, the only rudder to their journey.

He had learned several lessons in Gotland, but Magnus also carried within him earlier lessons about being guided by fear. Lessons he wished he could explain … but he knew Adrian was in no mood to listen, even if he could think of the right words. Adrian's fear was over a millennium old, as well worn as a lucky charm, as vast as a fanatic's faith, and as refined as a philosophy. It would take a clever man to convince him otherwise, and Magnus was in no way clever.

"So, what do we do?" he asked instead.

"I don't know," Adrian said, a hint of panic in his voice. "Damn it all. Damn it all to—"

And then he stopped, his youthful, olive face twisting into something sly, almost cruel, as he contemplated the heaped body. Magnus, following his gaze, saw it then: one blistered foot twitched, as if in sleep. "Shit," he said.

"He's alive," Adrian breathed at the same time. "Fetch him, Magnus. We can bring him to the hospice."

"*Carry* him? Adrian, he stinks—"

But Magnus was silenced with a look, one he knew all too well. It was a look that brooked no argument; past experience had taught him that testing that resolve would unleash a torrent of violence and fury, ending only when Adrian regained his senses, for the erines of Gabriel Berger knew little of tiring and a great deal about punishing weakness. Adrian had softened over the centuries, but he was still Gabriel's creation. The possibility of failure, with all its horrifying repercussions, always brought out the worst in him, and how much more terrible would it be now?

Instead, Magnus nodded, and the look turned away, taking with it some of the tension of the moment. He handed his own satchel to Adrian and strode up the road to the limp body of the monk. Unshaven and sallow; days, perhaps weeks since he last washed. The white tunic of the Dominican order, worn and greying, bore brown streaks that Magnus fervently hoped were nothing more than mud. Taking a last breath of fresh air, he bent over and felt the man's thready pulse, then shouldered him, shaking out the habit as best he could to remove the fleas and lice. Adrian was already striding down the road, their bags bouncing on his shoulder, purposeful once more; Magnus fell into step after him and silently hoped that the hospice had some manner of bath.

THE HOSPICE DID NOT HAVE a bath. It did, however, have a room for washing, full cisterns, roaring fires, and plenty of novices to bring him buckets of hot water. It was with a sigh of pleasure that Magnus stripped naked and set to bathing, dunking the cloth again and again, scrubbing at skin and hair alike. He poured out an entire bucket over himself, relishing the warmth—when men smelled as bad as the monk, he knew from years of practice mere wiping would not suffice. Too, there was something about water. It seemed to carry away all unpleasantness; it seemed, at times, a kind of rebirth. After Gotland, he had heated the water to a boil and poured the simmering cascade over himself, and again, and again; the scalding had felt a kind of healing.

After the first such dousing, Adrian had walked out of the room and had not come back until daybreak.

But that was past now. Or so Adrian had said; had said too that this one last task would put the seal on it. They would be free, for a time, as they had been before … except that they had never been free as Magnus understood the word. There was Adrian's will, and there was Gabriel's hanging like a sword over them both. All his life since being made erin was a balancing act between these two, as constant and relentless as the stars.

He dried himself and dressed, wincing at the caked mud on his dove-grey hose, the road smells of his linen shirt and brown tunic, then sighed when he spotted the wine and salad they had left him. What he would not give right now to get roaring drunk. Three days in a boozy stupor, with a wench or even a comely man; Adrian had taught him some of the pleasures of the latter. That was healing as he'd known it, four damn centuries and still he missed it—

Like a child, he stuck his finger in the wine and tasted it, but as always, it tasted sour and his throat closed. To live so long had been a gift, one he had never regretted, even with Gotland; but it seemed a touch cruel that he should do so only to be constantly faced with delights he would never know, like trebbiano wine.

Instead, he made his way to the warren of small rooms set aside for travelers, crossing the moonlit courtyard and turning down one small hall and then another. The courtyard garden's sweetness trailed in after him, rosemary and comfrey mingling with the greasy smell of tallow candles. Elsewhere he knew there were sickrooms and rooms for foundlings. It was a bustling place, despite the emptiness of the surrounding countryside: more like a village sharing a common building.

And everywhere small, olive-skinned monks, darting to and fro. All in the brown robes of Franciscans, not Dominicans like their monk. There had been whispers when they had brought their monk in; he seemed to be a remarkable one. The hospice's prior had nearly spirited him away, but Adrian had intervened, insisting that the monk be placed in an adjoining room at their expense. Another thing that tasted sour to Magnus. They had little money on them as it was. To spend it housing a strange monk in his own room? In other circumstances, Adrian would have sneered at the very idea.

Oh, it all felt *wrong*, and they hadn't even reached Florence.

As he reached their rooms, Magnus caught the eye of a novice at the end of the hall—one of the ones who had brought him the hot water. The young man smiled shyly and bowed, then vanished into the shadows, but not without a curious glance at the last moment. Few openly recoiled from Magnus's kind, but it was common to sense a careful distance in the men they dealt with. Open curiosity? Now, that was a rare trait indeed. Wide brown eyes and chestnut curls … too young for his tastes, but perhaps Adrian —? It might ease matters if Magnus could find him someone to fuck; if nothing else, a sated Adrian was better at listening.

The first door revealed their own room, empty, the bed untouched. Sighing, he opened the second door, only to be struck by a wave of sweat and urine. Sickroom smells mingling with tallow smoke—marvelous. Adrian was seated on a little chair at the bedside, a smile on his lips, for the monk was awake. As Magnus entered, the monk turned to him, the candlelight revealing a gaunt face crowned by a sunburnt tonsure, with clear grey eyes that seemed to bore straight into him, to see everything he kept within himself; the sensation made him shudder.

"Thanks be to God for enabling our prodigious encounter," the monk said, making the sign of the cross over him. "Truly, that we met under such circumstances shows His hand at work."

Magnus blinked, taken aback; he looked at Adrian, who was smiling beatifically. "Magnus, this is Fra Girolamo," he said. "He is bound for Florence, just as we are."

"Remarkable," Magnus said, "considering this is the road to Florence."

"I have been telling Fra Girolamo of our troubles," Adrian continued in the same honeyed tone. "Though soon, of course, we will have our audience with Signore Lorenzo and be restored our rightful property."

"Lorenzo il Magnifico can do anything, they say," Magnus agreed, leaning against the wall.

"My brothers," Fra Girolamo said, "You would do better to put your faith in God than in Lorenzo de' Medici. Whatever they say about him, he is but a man, and like all men, he can lose sight of God's truth in pursuit of his own desires." He spread his hands. "What is property compared to a man's soul?"

Magnus arched his eyebrows at Adrian: *Well?*

"But that is the very thing, Fra Girolamo," Adrian said, leaning forward with an earnest expression. "The book that was stolen from my father was one he had willed to our church. It was never intended for the shelves of the Medici. We thought surely Signore Lorenzo would not begrudge our humble village this one bequest, yet our letters have received no response."

For several heartbeats Fra Girolamo looked at Adrian. It was, to Magnus's eye, a measured look, not a sympathetic one. "Two men, seeking a book from Lorenzo de' Medici," he said slowly. "Now I understand …" He shook himself, then began pushing aside the thin blanket. "We shall pray for guidance."

Aghast, Magnus watched as Fra Girolamo eased himself out of the bed and knelt on the stone floor. Adrian's face lapsed briefly into pure exasperation, but when he caught Magnus's eye, he only jerked his finger at the floor, an order that brooked no argument, and lowered himself beside the monk.

Magnus got to his knees and folded his hands. The sickroom smell was worse now, closer to the blanket; he watched a bedbug crawl from wrinkle to wrinkle as the monk began praying in a low, driving Latin. Across the bed his gaze met Adrian's once more: he mouthed *Two days of this,* and Adrian shrugged and mouthed *Better plan,* and Magnus exhaled. Surely, thefts happened every day in Florence, what would be one more?

But there was Adrian's fear, steering them, and he had nothing to counter it.

At last the monk went back to sleep, and Magnus and Adrian returned to their own room. "How can a man pray for over an hour?" Adrian sat down on the sagging bed, the ropes creaking in protest, and began pulling off his boots. "How can he think of that much to say?"

"We cannot travel with him," Magnus said, sitting precariously on the lone chair. Everything in the hospice seemed designed for the skinny, stooped Franciscans, not his own oversized frame. "Even if we could persuade him to travel at night, he won't make Florence, Adrian, because I will kill him well before we get there."

He braced for Adrian's anger, but the latter only tittered. "Perhaps that's why his god brought us together—to make Fra Girolamo shut up once and for all." Suddenly, his head turned. "Is that someone in the hall? See if they're bringing him food."

Magnus went to the door and peeked out, then opened it completely. The shy novice paused, a tray clutched in his hands, and inclined his head. "God be with you, Signore."

"And with you. Is that for the friar?" Magnus inquired, smiling as the young man's cheeks flushed.

"A good broth, to help him regain his strength," the novice assented.

"Magnus, I want a word with him," Adrian called.

"If you could come in for a moment," Magnus said, stepping aside to let the novice in. His smile broadened as he saw Adrian do a double take, and the novice's flush deepened.

"I just wanted you to know that Fra Girolamo is sleeping," Adrian explained, his voice gentle. "But please, put that down for a moment and rest. You've been on your feet all day; I can tell."

At the latter, the novice's face became an alarming shade of red, but he put the tray down on the rickety table and sat in the chair Magnus had vacated, his eyes on the floor. Adrian stretched leisurely, then strolled over to the tray and bent over it, fanning the steam to his nostrils and breathing deeply. "It smells marvelous," he purred. "Did you make this?"

"No, Signore," the novice gasped. But he did not raise his eyes, and thus only Magnus saw Adrian quickly nip at his forefinger, then squeeze a few drops of his blood into the wine. Just enough to put a flush back into the monk's gaunt, sickly face; Magnus tried to imagine a truly robust Fra Girolamo and failed.

"Yet you are taking such good care of Fra Girolamo," Adrian said. "We are grateful for all that you and your brothers have done for us."

He was standing close to the novice, so close. The novice raised his eyes, only to stare at the gathered skirt of Adrian's doublet. "Perhaps you could bring us some as well," Adrian continued. "After you finish your tasks?"

"I—I will tell them, Signore—"

"I would prefer that you bring it yourself," Adrian interrupted in the same gentle voice. "Though if duty prevents you, I shall not take it as an insult."

The novice opened his mouth and closed it, fishlike, his heart-beat loud in the little room. Despite himself, Magnus's fangs were poking from his gums in anticipation. He had fed on the road, he had no real appetite as such; but oh, the novice was like a succulent fruit, all but dripping with juices. Ages since he'd had anyone so young. Ages, too, since he'd had another soul look at him with real desire—

"May I bring the tray to Fra Girolamo now?" the novice asked, his voice trembling.

With a flourish Adrian stepped back, letting the novice take up the tray once more. He went to the door but stopped again and asked in a squeak, "Is it true?"

Magnus looked at Adrian, but the latter made a cutting gesture. "Is what true, my brother?"

"Fra Girolamo. Is he the one they speak of? From Bologna? Who has been given visions by God?" The novice's eyes were alight with excitement. "Is he Savonarola?"

Adrian stared at him, astonished; and then he shrugged, all

gentle flirtation gone. "I have no idea," he said. "Why don't you ask him yourself?"

The novice didn't seem to notice the change in Adrian's tone; he bowed and darted from the room. As soon as he was gone, Adrian's face became a mask of fury. For a moment he stood there, trembling, fangs jutting from his mouth, breath hissing in his throat; had they been more isolated, Magnus knew, the furniture would have been kicked to kindling. At last he drew his fangs up and pointed at Magnus. "Pack your things. We leave at sundown."

"The monk no longer suits?" Magnus asked mildly.

"If he's deliberately given himself such a reputation, he'll be more interested in allying with Lorenzo than aiding our cause. If he's a fanatic and figures out what we are, we could end up facing a mob." Adrian shook his head, fuming. "All the bloody monks in the world and I get the one with visions, who's already so infamous they've heard his name in this shithole of a hospice. We've wasted a night and the price of two rooms. Why aren't you packing?"

"Because he still may be of use," Magnus continued in the same mild tone. "If he's infamous, Lorenzo will certainly want to meet him when he arrives; hell, Lorenzo probably sent for him in the first place. Two followers in his wake would not be closely inspected."

Adrian scowled but said nothing.

"Or are you just angry because that novice prefers to sit at the monk's bedside rather than let you test his faith?"

Adrian kicked Magnus, but it was a glancing blow, his anger settling into a pout. Magnus grinned. "And I see I *divined* correctly …"

"Do *not* pun, Magnus. Your puns are excruciating." But a smile was tugging at Adrian's mouth. "Besides, I thought my whole plan was moot, as you would murder him before we set foot in the city?"

"Was that a plan? I thought that was just a passing fancy, like when you bought that blue hose that stained your legs." Before Adrian could reply, he continued. "We can go ahead, arrange to cross his path again in Florence—"

"Oh, no, no, Magnus. We couldn't do *that*. If we leave without him, he'll set out on foot again, and the next time he drops, he won't get up." Adrian grinned at him. "No, Magnus, your superior wisdom has convinced me. We shall hire a cart, and we shall deliver this monk to Florence ourselves, the better to be received by Lorenzo il Magnifico."

Magnus frowned, going over their conversation in his mind. "Did I—did I just fuck myself?"

"Unless we can hire that novice to drive us, and then he can fuck us both." Adrian went to the window, pressing his face to the crack between the shutters. "Half the night gone already," he mused. "He won't be ready tomorrow … Two, even three days before we could leave … They won't be in a hurry to release him if they think him some kind of prophet …" He tapped the wood as he thought. "No, Magnus, you may be right yet again, though it is agony for me to admit it. Our monk's usefulness lies in Florence. We'll leave money for his transportation, to ensure he makes it there in one piece. You and I will go ahead. I don't want to alarm the infamous Savonarola with our habits, and I want to make sure none of our fellows are near enough to interfere. Too many of the dangenes bank with Florentines, and would love an excuse to pick a fight with Gabriel … and then there's our own erines to contend with. We'll ask some questions on the road and fine-tune our tale of woe for Fra Girolamo. Surely, he'll intercede on behalf of those who showed him such generosity."

Magnus frowned. "What if he vanishes inside a monastery and refuses to see us?"

"Oh, that one will never hide away. He needs an audience, no matter his intent." Adrian barked with laughter. "'Visions from God!' That novice was practically panting at the thought. Can you imagine the arrogance, to think the divine speaks to you directly?"

"I can not only imagine it, I've smelled it up close," Magnus muttered.

"And your suffering is noted. Do you want to spend the day here or leave now?"

"If we spend an entire day here, Adrian, you won't keep your hands to yourself—and then all the novices will be whispering about your icy affection."

"Only one novice, Magnus; I abhor a crowd, as well you know. Too many things sticking into too many places; I get distracted." He counted off his fingers. "So, you to pack and find the quickest egress from this place, I to the stables to arrange something for our monk."

"By *arrange*, of course, you mean tupping that novice."

"Who said anything about tupping? I am only thinking to comfort a poor young man, who has nothing to entertain himself but prayer and servitude." When Magnus only scowled, Adrian rose up on his toes and kissed him wetly on the cheek. "Next time, we'll be sure to stop at a nunnery," he said, and slipped out into the hall.

THEY LEFT the hospice a few hours before dawn, a pile of coins and a scribbled note of instructions on the table, then over the wall to avoid the dozing guard at the gate, their departure witnessed only by the rows of shuttered windows like so many reptilian eyes. Outside, the moon hung clear and bright in the vast bowl of the sky, the stars an explosion of light across the blackness, and Magnus felt himself ease with each step. The monk had irritated him, and monasteries unnerved him. There was always an undercurrent, different flavors of frustration and appetite; he knew too much about both to rest calmly in its presence.

Nunneries: now, that was a different matter entirely. Frustrated novices in nunneries. The thought made him smile, but he quickly banished the images from his mind. Adrian was swinging from tense to amused and back again, and Magnus knew to tread carefully. Even his tryst in the stables had not completely unwound him. Nearly a year since Gotland now. Time had changed once Magnus was made erin: the years felt like months, even weeks sometimes … but he was starting to think that Gotland had marked them permanently. For four centuries he had watched Adrian slowly shed the cruel servant Magnus had first known. That he might retreat to that again—oh, Magnus couldn't bear to think it.

They didn't have to do this. There had been no express order to retrieve this book; it had been a request, the kind of thing Gabriel did from time to time, the better to watch his erines fight like dogs to further win favor. *It would please me to have it, at any price save suspicion.* The *please* alone had kept Adrian awake for days, trying to tease out all the possibilities. But they didn't want to be dogs—or at least Magnus did not. Gotland had shown him he could be driven to that, as so many had before him. Months of such abuse? He would be clamoring to lick Gabriel's shoes, wipe his ass, anything to be treated with something less than that unending viciousness. Adrian had decided the book could buy them further respite, that fawning obedience plus winning Gabriel his prize would earn them another period of grace. *It would please me.* But Magnus thought it best to stay out of mind, forgotten—and there was also the simple logistics of delivery.

If Adrian walked into that castle again, Magnus feared he would never, ever come out.

"Who else do you think will try for it?" he asked.

Adrian blinked, lost in his own thoughts, then looked up at him. "Of our fellows? I'm not certain. Seissan definitely, and he'll be clever about it. He knows how men work and he has ambition enough for all of us. Gemma may well have a go, to spite Seissan if nothing else. Thaddeus is far enough, I think, that he can ignore it without losing face. Ihsan? I cannot say, but I can never say with her …"

"Vincent?"

Adrian snorted. "Never. If he's pushed to it, he'll send one of his own erines, no matter the risk." His expression softened then. "He has survived this long by cowering, and I cannot say as I blame him. But we know now what hiding can lead to."

"Adrian," Magnus began carefully, "we cannot let Gabriel rule our every action—"

"Magnus," Adrian cut in, "he is *my* genetes. Ruling me is the bedrock he built me on."

"But you are more than that. You were more than that when he found you, and you are still more than that." Magnus stopped in the road, trying to catch Adrian's eye. "Just think around him, as we've always done. If Seissan wins the book instead of us, would it not be as much a distraction? He'll use it to be made cagè, perhaps even cifet, and the Skìa will hate him for rising so quickly; the infighting alone will entertain Gabriel for months. And Seissan may be an asshole, but he's an asshole who can be bargained with. It could serve our purpose just as well to help him."

Adrian frowned. "I will think on it," he said curtly, turning to walk—

"Adrian, we cannot go back to Gotland," Magnus said. "Not so soon. It doesn't matter what you bring him. It will be a flag in front of a bull."

"I'm not asking *you* to go back, Magnus." He spat the words out. "This is between myself and Gabriel. You're merely a moment of *my* weakness, remember? A lapse of *my* judgment, a waste of *my* blood and thus *his* blood, and he can only indulge so much. Four centuries he waited to use that one against us, and I'm only surprised he didn't hold out longer. His games are long, Magnus— as I should know," he pressed as Magnus started to speak, his voice rising to a whine. "You might say I know him inside and out. So I will ask, *my* creation, that you defer to *my* expertise, especially as you won't be taking any risk?"

Every word a slap. Magnus looked away, swallowing hard to keep his throat from closing. Too far, he had gone too far. He knew

Adrian was speaking out of fear, that he didn't—he *couldn't*—mean to hurt him. It didn't make it any easier to listen to.

And before Gotland, Adrian would have noticed his response; noticed it and bridged the gap between them with an apology, a touch, even if he would brook no more discussion. But his genetes was already well down the road, his dark hair bouncing and his boots slapping the packed earth of the road, striding with single-minded purpose toward Florence.

2

Magnus could not stop looking.

Despite the late hour, the road leading to Florence was unusually crowded, and Adrian was muttering anxiously about getting through the gate before curfew. But the slope in the road let them see over the walls into the city itself … and the cathedral's dome, towering within. The dome was enormous, gigantic, beyond language. Every time he forced himself to look away, his gaze would return to it, as if bewitched by its scale; it was so impossibly vast, he wondered if he was still dreaming. His slumber had been abruptly severed by Adrian's kick; they had slept nearly until nightfall and the gates would be closing and why hadn't Magnus remembered? Cutting across plowed fields while tying their cloaks against the spitting rain, and suddenly there had been that great reddish half-circle like a setting sun. Where else had he seen something that massive? He couldn't remember. He had seen castles and palaces aplenty in his time … but here, now, on this Tuscan road quickly becoming mud, the dome seemed grander than anything he could recall. When he had first described their task to Magnus, Adrian had included the cathedral in the list of the Medici's accomplishments, part of assessing their adversary. The dome may have been Brunelleschi's creation, but it was Medici money and canniness that had gotten the building completed, as the Medici had shaped so much of Florence in just three generations.

For the first time since they had set out, Magnus wondered if *Il Magnifico* wasn't a stupid moniker after all but truly deserved.

Adrian, he knew, was not looking at the dome. The wonders of the moment held little interest for him; somewhere in Adrian's mind, his mortal past had become a sun-bright, perfect idyll, a pinnacle of all aspects of mankind from art to society to warfare to lovemaking, and everything else was but a tawdry echo. No matter that his memories were a millennium old now. Even this dome would be declared insignificant when compared to some achievement in Adrian's time, though Magnus refused to believe it. It seemed some kind of otherworldly act; it seemed impossible that it could be the product of a single man's mind and not some expression of the whole of humanity. But when he looked at Adrian's face, forever youthful and world-weary at once, his hazel eyes were indeed locked on a more mundane sight.

Fra Girolamo's cart was about a dozen paces ahead of them, making its way toward the gates, the monk himself upright beside the driver and blessing everyone around him, because that was what monks did to pass the time, Magnus supposed. They had been careful to keep a group of merchants between them, shielding them in case the monk turned around, but he was too busy blessing everything: families that ran up to him as he passed, fellow travelers, the cart-driver, the horses, the cart, the pigs that someone was driving in the ditch beside the road. Did pigs go to heaven? Magnus didn't remember seeing them in any fresco of that cloudy world, nor horses for that matter, and horses had more uses. It seemed ridiculous to raise up, say, the rotund little merchant riding within arm's reach—who had been nattering on and on about some slave girl he had fucked, should he have bought her for his own?—and not the beast he rode on, who suffered the asshole's presence with a nobility of spirit few men could achieve. Here, Magnus decided, was an argument to disprove the very idea of a heaven: the horse lumbering through a kind of horsey purgatory for no spiritual reward, while her rider verbally shat in every ear that had the misfortune to hear him, yet could buy his salvation whenever he pleased.

Adrian, of course, noticed none of this. He was watching the cart with a hawklike intensity; Magnus could all but see the plans forming and re-forming behind his beetled brows. They were drawing close to the gate—just another city gate, it could have been anywhere, clearly they hadn't set Brunelleschi to their design—and the traffic slowed as everyone funneled through the opening. Now Magnus saw two guards waving them through and the first red-roofed buildings past the city wall, and he felt a twinge of *wrongness* deep in his belly—was it his lingering awe at the dome, or something else?

Suddenly, Adrian seized his arm, his fingers digging into Magnus's flesh. Alarmed, Magnus looked down at him. "What is it?"

"There," Adrian said, the word a growl. He jerked his chin towards the gate.

Magnus peered ahead, trying to glimpse faces, weapons, what was he looking for? "I don't see anything."

The fingers dug deeper, making him wince with pain. "Seissan," Adrian ground out. "Ahead. The black cloak."

Again Magnus looked, but his stomach was knotting. They had been through every inn and stable, spoken to everyone they passed between the hospice and here, and found not a hint of another erin. Black cloak? There had to be more than a dozen black cloaks on the road. Seissan was small and dark; so were half the men around them. "I cannot smell him," he said carefully. "And there was nothing in any of the inns we passed."

"And yet he's here, Magnus," Adrian retorted, his voice rising. "Which means he knows how close we are; he'll find a way—"

But he broke off as one of the black-cloaked figures turned around to say something to another man, revealing a flushed, all-too-human face. "I was mistaken," he muttered, dropping his hand.

"An understandable mistake," Magnus said soothingly. "But you cannot become distracted. That is precisely the kind of uncertainty the others thrive on. If anyone gets close, we'll know and we'll act accordingly."

Still Adrian's face remained grim. "I want to catch the monk before the gate," he said, as if Magnus hadn't spoken at all. But just then, the damp procession ground to a halt as the pigs suddenly merged into the road, the animals rooting around people's legs while they exclaimed and kicked clods of mud at the massive beasts. Arguments broke out, the guards hurried forward, people tried to move horses and carts around the chaos and succeeded in blocking the road further. The air filled with a clamor of complaining voices, punctuated by a shriek as one of the pigs wiggled under an old woman's skirts.

"Best fun she's had in ages, eh? Face like that's only fit for a pig," the nattering merchant said, and then laughed his nasally little laugh. The sound made Magnus's nerves jangle; he took a step closer to the man but stopped at Adrian's warning hiss. The raised voices of the crowd rang out around them, echoing off the walls, and Adrian hissed again as a voice bellowed for more guards to come.

Ahead of them Fra Girolamo leapt nimbly off his cart and waded in among the pigs. He spoke to the guards, he spoke to the pig-herder, he blessed everyone and started praying, and, miraculously, everyone started praying too. It was as if a blanket of calm had been laid over the road and everyone on it; when the rain began in earnest, it seemed only to underscore the monk's driving voice, the thudding Latin syllables echoed by the splattering drops. Everyone bowed their heads in that shared moment—all, that is, save for the nattering merchant.

"You know," he said to one of his companions, leaning over to nudge him when the man didn't look up, "I've seen things in monasteries you would not believe! I was staying at one outside of Milan, right? And this cart pulls up, just like that one there, and it looks like it's carrying more monks, but I said to myself something's not right. And sure enough, under those robes were six of the most poxy whores ..."

Magnus noted the slack reins in the man's hand, the way he was straining out of the saddle to keep his companion's attention; saw too the horse's swishing tail and wide eyes. He drew the smallest of his knives from his bag, gripping it so just the tip of the blade was jutting from his fist, and stepped close to them. The horse's head turned as she regarded him, her dark eye seeming to say *get this fucker off me.*

"... all these noises coming from the chancel, and when I go to look, you wouldn't believe it! A line of backsides and these randy old men swinging their little whips ..."

His voice had risen above the prayer, and people were starting to look; Adrian glanced at Magnus, saw the knife in his hand, and rolled his eyes.

"... whipping them while giving themselves a tugging! You would have thought they were six of the king's mistresses, not the dregs of Milan ..."

The monk pronounced "amen" in a ringing voice as the crowd surged toward him, reaching to kiss his hand, his robe. Adrian began pushing forward, the natterer blathering on about grunting monks and squealing whores; Magnus mouthed a silent apology to the horse and cut open his palm. The smell of his blood made the horse shy away with a whinny; the natterer, already unbalanced, yelped in surprise as he toppled out of the saddle, but Magnus was already well up the road. He heard a muddy crash and a louder cry of fear, the sounds of horses stomping and being quieted, the other merchants heaping invectives on the natterer for not controlling his mount.

He licked both hand and knife clean, the wound already closing, wondering if the natterer would get a kicking as well. It would have made a good wager, if Adrian had been in a better mood. But there was to be no wagering today: ahead of him, Adrian's arms were already thrown out in feigned delight as he greeted Fra Girolamo. For a moment, a fleeting expression of resignation crossed the monk's face, but before Magnus could wonder at it he was bowing beside Adrian, and when he looked up again Fra Girolamo was piously signing the cross over them, his expression placid once more. Again Magnus felt that ache of wrongness. What would the monk make of it, he wondered. Perhaps it was just what people felt when approaching so much holiness. Like a chill in the room.

"Thanks be to God, that He brings us together once more," Fra Girolamo said, smiling beneath his hood made limp from rain.

"It is a blessing to see you in such good health again," Adrian replied, his smile so broad, Magnus wondered if it was hurting him.

"All thanks to God," the monk said.

And our money, Magnus thought.

People were hurrying through the gates once more, eager to get inside and escape the rain; the cart driver beckoned to Fra Girolamo, who in turn said to Adrian, "You will of course stay with me at the convent and allow me to repay your hospitality."

The surprise vanished from Adrian's face as soon as it appeared; he bowed again and Magnus did the same. "I thank you," Adrian said when he straightened, his face beaming gratitude and sorrow in equal measure. "The road has not been kind to us, though we will see our journey through to the end."

Again that ache in Magnus's belly; again he pushed it away. Nothing more than hunger pangs, for what could this monk stand to gain by keeping them close?

"Then it is settled." Fra Girolamo began climbing onto the cart, and at a nudge from Adrian, Magnus helped him up. At least in the rain their hands were equally cold. "I cannot offer you luxury, but our rooms are dry, our food nourishing, and our spirituality uplifting to all who seek refuge."

His voice was smooth, authoritative, with some of the driving force of his prayer; Magnus gave Adrian a look as they hopped onto the back of the cart, but the latter's eyes were demurely downcast. "If we would not be too much trouble."

"It will be no trouble," Fra Girolamo said, gesturing at the grey clouds. "Everything is as God wills it."

Like a fool, Magnus followed his pointing arm upward, only to get rain in his eyes. God was taking the piss, perhaps literally; but Adrian looked calm at last, and he would take his mercies where he could find them.

And thus they entered Florence: two beings far closer to demons than men, this holiest of monks, and a driver who placidly farted close to Magnus's face as the cart wobbled over a hole in the road. The guards barely gave them a glance.

THE RAINY DARKNESS had blotted out all detail, so all Magnus saw upon entering Florence were yet more fields that gave way to a haze of buildings and huddled figures, shuttered lights and grey-black mist ... until they came to the convent, its elegant church serving as punctuation to a building otherwise as featureless as a curtain wall. Another monastery, smelling of men and their blind faith, and their greed as well. Once inside, the first fresco they had seen had a sky of such vivid blue, it had hurt Magnus's eyes, even in torchlight. Ground gemstones and gilded halos; more Medici money, it seemed. It had taken him all of an eyeblink to ascertain that many of San Marco's faithful did not want this particular monk in their convent. He was, apparently, too much monk even for them. There had been a whispered argument over a particularly opulent cell for one of the older brothers, though why anyone should begrudge an old man a silk-trimmed woolen blanket and a rug on the tiled floor, Magnus couldn't say. The place felt cool even to him, which meant in winter it would be freezing, and half the

monks looked to have rheumatism, gout, or some other debili-
tating condition. Surely, God hadn't meant His lads to suffer this
much—

And then he saw the hairshirt and scourge Fra Girolamo had
requested for his personal use, and, well. Clearly, Magnus had
misunderstood their god's wishes.

They were shown to two plain rooms side by side, with narrow
beds and rough wool blankets. Each room, however, had wax
candles and a fresco on the wall. Patronage, one of the monks had
explained at their surprise; the Medici had been beloved patrons of
San Marco since Cosimo. Fra Girolamo's face twisted at the words,
but he had said nothing. In Magnus's room, the fresco showed a
crowned Mary, radiant; she reminded Magnus of a woman he had
lain with, but then, many faces reminded him of others, so much
variety and yet in the end all blurring together with the years.

Crowned like a queen. Far to the west there was a queen,
Denèter, who ruled over all the dangenes, Gabriel included. Her
court more powerful than the Berger court ... *and with four more
dangenes to cope with*, Adrian had said, *so five times the scheming, five
times the cruelty, five times the appeasement. You put women on
pedestals, Magnus; remember Gabriel withdrew to Gotland not because
of the others' condemnation but because Denèter was having all the fun.*
The *fun* said with that bitter humor that they all shared, the erines
of Gabriel, because to try and find proper words for what Gabriel
did, for what all his people did, was to face that horror, and one did
not survive centuries by facing anything.

But these were dark thoughts, and he knew better than to
follow them. Adrian could not control his melancholy; it was
Magnus's job to keep his own restrained. He checked the door
bolts: easy to break if need be. He strode up and down the hall,
giving Adrian a brief nod as he eyed the windows, the doors on
either end, the loggia they had passed through. The courtyard was
airy and open; the walls scalable without fuss. Hopefully, though,
all his precautions were naught; hopefully, they would sleep

through the day, then stroll over to wherever Lorenzo lived, steal the book, and leave.

Hopefully.

When he returned to his room, Adrian was waiting, and for once he was truly beaming, not just performing for the monk. "Tomorrow, in the evening," he announced, waving at Magnus to shut the door. "He will bring us to the Palazzo Medici and introduce us. We may not get a private audience—you were right, Magnus; Lorenzo asked for this monk specifically to return to Florence, something about a cardinal brother needing guidance— but at the very least, we can survey the doors, the guards, everything."

Magnus nodded. "But only a meeting means another night to steal it, perhaps longer if we cannot pinpoint its location." *Perhaps a blessing in disguise*, he added silently.

"It may," Adrian concurred. "But we have an advantage now, Magnus." At Magnus's frown, his smile broadened. "We have God on our side."

Magnus sniggered despite himself, and Adrian burst out laughing; and then they looked at each other, Adrian still dabbing at his eyes. Unspoken between them was the acknowledgment: this was the first joke Adrian had made since Gotland. Not black humor, not sarcasm, but just a silly, terrible joke; it felt, for a moment, like they'd already succeeded.

AT FRA GIROLAMO'S URGING, they joined the early-morning service, sitting as far back as they dared with their heads bowed, contemplating the richly polished wood of the pews and their own dirty fingernails. The air smelled of incense and damp wool and wax, a combination Magnus had come to associate with religion. He and Adrian fidgeted to hide their exhausted yawns, pretending to have just awakened after a few hours' rest. Still, the monks'

singing washed over Magnus like that first bath after Gotland, soothing his unease, smoothing away the *wrongness* ... until, suddenly, the Eucharist was brought forth and the monks all turned to them as if of one mind. Watching, keenly; watching too keenly. Why were they being offered communion? He looked at Adrian and saw the same surprise on his face, barely masked by that ridiculous smile that Magnus wanted to slap: he was so tired, and now this. The two of them walking up the aisle, a monk before and after them like they were prisoners. On their knees again. All because of Adrian's fear. Magnus flattened the bread in the roof of his mouth with his tongue, his stomach cramping at the mere taste. Bile jumping up and down his throat; back in the safety of the pew, he dabbed his mouth with his sleeve, pushing the spit-soft bread into the folds of linen, and saw Adrian do the same.

Their monk was scheming; Magnus knew it now. His driving voice as he preached, his eyes alight with a strange fervor—oh, Magnus understood why they had heard of him at the hospice, why the monks here at San Marco either feared or adored him. He wore a clean white gown under a new black robe, and it seemed to flash as he spoke, though the chapel was dim and cool. As if he were lit from within. Magnus's experiences with preaching were admittedly few, but in all his years, he had never heard this kind of energetic declaration at the altar. Many spoke the words, even passionately, but Fra Girolamo exuded a flavor of conviction that reminded Magnus of soldiers just before the start of battle. Not just faith but something more: it was as if this beady-eyed man truly believed he was a direct conduit of the divine.

And what would this God have to say about the likes of Adrian and himself?

They were finally allowed to retire to their rooms, Adrian pleading the weariness of the road. Once his door was shut and the hall outside empty, Magnus spat and spat into his chamber pot, cleaning the taste from his mouth, then scraped the bread into it and shoved the pot far under the bed. He lay down, twitching with exhaustion and restlessness, too tired for sleep now. All the permutations, all the possible outcomes of their search jumbled in his mind, refusing to untangle themselves into logical plans and consequences; too, he kept feeling the stone beneath his knees, the sensation of looking up into Fra Girolamo's cool grey stare. The longer he tossed and turned, the smaller the room felt, until at last he couldn't take it anymore and slipped back outside.

The hall was bright with afternoon sunlight, but thankfully, it wasn't beating directly into the gallery; he wasn't sure how he would explain the blisters and swelling. Perhaps they would think it a miracle; perhaps they would simply drag him out into the blinding heat and sing hymns over his bubbling flesh. In the courtyard, two monks were tending carefully to a little patch of garden, snipping the last tender greens and turning over a section of earth, churning up smells of rosemary and rich soil, the latter odor as pleasurable as food had once been. Magnus moved swift and silent along the gallery and back into the dim, cool chapel, the only other place he could think of to go. Without the monks, it was quiet and somber, almost tomb-like, and welcoming in its silence; strange how the absence of men removed all the wrongness. As if he could now see it clearly, see past the fat of the monks to the bones of the room, and take comfort in it.

Not the worst thing, this religion, if it made spaces like this. Oh, he would have preferred a woman to tumble with, or at least a mouthful of fresh blood to soothe the ache in his belly, but this would do. From the pew he had a clear view of the altarpiece, now visible for not having Fra Girolamo gesticulating in front of it. Another Mary, this time with her infant and many admirers, the figures lifelike despite the thick gold halos weighting their heads. The more he gazed at it, the more he felt embarrassed, as if he were an interloper spying on a private gathering. Too, there was something familiar about the scene—the rug especially tugged at his mind; he was certain he had stood on something similar once, somewhere. So many memories now; too many for his mind to keep.

Everyone was so serious. Was it not supposed to be a source of joy, this infant? Shouldn't they be dancing, celebrating? Hairshirts and frigid cells: why did they persist in making it all so dour? Wasn't there enough suffering in the world, that they had to work to create more?

Still, it was better than Gotland. Sucking bread on his knees and the judgment of divine toddlers: irritating, humiliating, and yet delightful in comparison to Gotland. Fra Girolamo should visit Gotland; he would learn a great deal about suffering, far beyond a few slaps of his whip. Suffering, and kneeling, too. The thought pleased Magnus: send the monk to Gotland with the book while they stayed here with Mary. Now, there was someone worth kneeling before, he would take quite a few things from her pretty hands; oh, he would swallow all without protest and then see if he could return the favor—

He shook himself and looked around furtively. The last thing they needed was for a monk to find him in the chapel with a stiff cock. Instead, he forced his eyes down to the pew before him and set himself to thinking through the evening. They would need to locate where Lorenzo kept his books, but important too would be to count the guards, determine all the entrances and exits, and were there adjoining properties? Here the buildings were cheek by jowl, but if the palazzo was closer to the city walls, it might be surrounded by open space …

A voice cleared, startling him, and he turned to see Fra Girolamo standing at the end of the pew. Inwardly Magnus groaned. He was no good at this sort of thing; he always let Adrian do the talking. He started to rise, but the monk waved him back down, and he silently groaned again.

"I thought perhaps we could speak a little," Fra Girolamo said, settling beside him. He smelled cleaner than the road, but only just;

the white robe already had a dirty hem. "You serve your master well."

Magnus inclined his head. He was trying to think; he could not think. These were the situations he inevitably botched. He would make a muck of it, and Adrian would be furious, and all this would have been for nothing—

"Only I fear the weight he has given this task," the monk continued, speaking slowly. "I just invited him to accompany me to the palazzo now rather than later, but he would not hear of changing our appointment."

He looked at Magnus expectantly, and Magnus's stomach clenched. He managed a little shrug: *What can I say? My master's an ass.*

"Many have been taught, erroneously, that the path to salvation lies in the correct gifts to God." His voice was starting to take on the rhythm of the pulpit. "But such exchanges are a stratagem of the devil; the true path lies in the heart, and the goodness of our deeds." He laid a hairy hand atop Magnus's before he could move away, yet the monk seemed oblivious to the chill of his flesh. "Your master, I think, fears for his soul, and that fear is addling his reason. If you could indicate to me the contours of his sin, I could guide him to true repentance."

Magnus gaped at him, astonished; and then he nearly laughed aloud. The contours of Adrian's sins? They were like a mountain range, jagged peaks of violence and valleys of depravity. For a moment, he indulged in the vision of starting such a tale, and Fra Girolamo's reaction: would he seize up and die of shock? Would he bellow for the stake and the bonfire, or perhaps the gallows, or just a dozen stout axes? Many had called them demon, lacking a more precise lexicon for their evil: what would Fra Girolamo do if he knew there were hundreds of such demons in the world, serpent-sired and wholly corrupted, and their very blood miraculous?

"Most pious friar," he said, choosing his words with care, "I cannot say what drives my master. Even I do not know what truly lies in his heart. But I too fear what will come of us not retrieving the book. To have it returned, I think, would ease much pain and grief, and perhaps allow my master to see ... other matters, more clearly."

And there it was again: that knowing stare, as if he saw something Magnus himself could not. "Then we shall pray that your master gets the outcome he deserves," he said, bowing his head over his clasped hands.

Magnus did the same. His heart was beating steadily, as if threatened; the bile taste was back. *Salvation lies in the correct gifts to God.* It was closer to the mark than he liked to hear from a stranger; it was closer to the mark than he liked to think about, period. He had thought the better path was to let Seissan, or another, have the book, and focus on staying away from Gotland. Now, his thoughts untangling themselves at last, he wondered if Adrian's fear would simply not accept that outcome, would choose to read it as doom no matter how Magnus reasoned it out for him. For the first time, he understood, with a sudden flash of insight, that not knowing Gabriel's mind might kill Adrian, whether by outright suicide or just frightening himself into the grave.

That returning to Gotland might be the less-maddening option for Adrian—oh, it threatened to drive Magnus mad in turn. Worse than a dog returning to its own sick. Adrian would argue his case to the point of fury, would remind Magnus again and again that he wasn't there when the original erines rebelled, he didn't know what it was like, he could never imagine the utter hell Gabriel unleashed upon them ... but Magnus had been in the cellars of Gotland now. And while he still dreamed of it, still woke in cold sweats from it and jumped at certain noises and watched for the black cloaks of Gabriel's Skìa, all as mad as their master—

Despite all of that, he was willing to fight to keep away from Gotland—or, better yet, to destroy Gabriel. But he knew that Adrian would never again attempt the latter.

Beside him, Fra Girolamo raised his head, exhaling long and

low, a satisfied sound. He looked at Magnus and smiled. "You may not believe it, but God is speaking, always. Everyone serves His plan—no matter their true nature."

Magnus nodded, a cursory gesture. The only voice he served was Adrian's, and the only voice Adrian served was Gabriel's, a chain of blood as solid as those of iron. Still his heart thudded in his chest, even after Fra Girolamo took his leave and the chapel was quiet once more. It was some time before the peace of the space descended again, and when it did, it felt different: cheaper, less real. At last, weary, Magnus rose and looked at the altarpiece one last time.

"I'm sorry for how Gotland went," he muttered. "I'm sorry for all of it."

Mary didn't respond, just kept gazing at her son with the same half-lidded gaze as before. *It's just a picture*, Magnus told himself, *stop being foolish*. But still, he glanced back one last time at the chapel door, as if even the likes of himself might be worthy of a miracle.

3

MAGNUS DREAMED THROUGH THE AFTERNOON, contorting in the narrow bed to avoid the sunlight that found its way through the shutters. Above him, Mary rose from her pretty throne and stepped into the room, and he knelt at her feet as she poured blood from a golden chalice into his waiting mouth. *The blood of the lamb*, she said, and he felt he was being given a profound gift; but when the blood touched his tongue, it was as dry and crumbling as the bread had been. He tried to close his mouth but he couldn't, his jaws were being held open and that beautiful exquisite face kept smiling at him as she poured and poured the red sand into him, he was drowning and her robes were not radiant blue but black and her fangs glistened inches from his face and he knew then it had all been a terrible trick and he had fallen for it, he had lost himself and Adrian both, now Adrian would suffer for him again and they would never ever leave Gotland—

He awoke parched and gagging, his face wedged against the wall, flecks of plaster smeared on his lips and the mattress so distorted, he could feel the ropes beneath. It took him several heartbeats to place himself, to understand the voices murmuring in

Tuscan and Latin as they passed outside his door, to remember that he was in Florence on a fool's errand.

The tiles were cool beneath his feet as he swung himself upright, his toes just outside the shaft of late afternoon sunlight streaking in. Still early; would this day never end? A bell tolled for some reason and there was a flurry of footsteps without, the voices excited now. Being called to a meal, a prayer? He had a sudden, odd urge to join them, to go outside and fall in among them, trading the little information of the day. Work, prayer, food, sleep. There were worse fates.

There were worse fates, and Adrian had spared him such.

As he thought this, there was a rustle at the door; yawning, he went and opened it, ready for an exhausted Adrian or a frenetic one —but it was only a monk, one hand raised to knock, the other cradling a mound of folded black and white garments topped by a pair of dirty sandals, which he now held out to Magnus.

"From Fra Girolamo," the monk explained.

Magnus stared at the robe, blinking. "Pardon?"

"It is laundry day tomorrow," the monk explained. "Fra Girolamo invites you to include your clothes for washing." He gestured to a basket in the hall. "When you have dressed, you can place your clothes in the basket."

Magnus blinked again. "That is kind of him," he managed, "but we are being introduced to Lorenzo de' Medici—"

"Indeed," the monk said, and held out the habit and sandals with a patient expression.

Now truly confused, Magnus looked up and down the hall: no one. There was only the monk, the basket, and the clothes being held out to him; he took them. The monk bowed and turned away.

"Wait." Magnus touched his cheek, now bristling. "What about a shave?"

The monk frowned. "It is not shaving day today," he said, as if Magnus should know this.

"Is there a—" *barber nearby*, he was going to say, but the monk had already walked away, taking measured steps down the hall and out into the sunlit courtyard, not once looking back.

Magnus went to Adrian's door and opened it without knocking. He shut it behind himself, tossed the habit and sandals next to the identical set on the floor, and wiggled onto the bed beside Adrian's coverlet-swathed form.

"What the fuck are the clothes for?" he asked wearily.

"Something about presenting to Lorenzo," cane the muffled reply, punctuated by a yawn. "He wanted to go there at the most ridiculous hour."

"He wants us to dress as novices to see Lorenzo." Magnus scowled at the clothing, as if he could wrest from it an explanation. "Why does he want us to dress as novices?"

"Who cares? It's as good a disguise as any." Adrian kicked his shin with a bare foot. "If you're sleeping here, mind how you lay. Mice have been at the ropes; it's a wonder they're holding us both up."

"Something's not right." But he could go no further; the sun was beating in through Adrian's shutters just as it had in his own room. He was still so tired. "First communion, and now these robes? He's plotting something, I know it."

"Maybe he thinks he can convert us," Adrian said, giggling. He nudged Magnus with his foot again. "You sound miserable. When did you last feed?"

He was drowsing, dozing. "Too long ago." Sliding around Adrian's familiar form, smelling him, a hundred thousand days spent thus—

"Well, behave yourself tonight. You can drink after we get the book. Not before."

Drink, Mary whispered, bending over him in the black doublet and hose of the Skìa. *Drink while you can, because you will never be free of him.*

"Unless I surprise him," he mumbled. He was asleep before Adrian could reply.

IN ADRIAN'S ROOM, the fresco was of yet another Mary holding yet another plump infant, this time pointing at the ceiling with a sour expression on his round little face; Magnus felt a kinship with this one, as he too felt quite sour. Adrian's habit fit him as if he were born to it, and the darkness of the cloak brought out the olive of his skin. Magnus's habit, on the other hand, was far too short in both hem and sleeves: his wrists and ankles stuck out like a bumpkin's, knobby and ghostly pale in the candlelight.

"He said something at midday about tensions in Florence, that two strange men might not be permitted to enter, but two novices …" Adrian turned one way and another, fiddling with the belt. "It's not like we haven't done it before."

"That's not the point. It's as if he were conspiring with us," Magnus said, trying and failing to pull the sleeves down farther. Too, every time he moved the long piece twisted and the belt rode up, and the two hoods—and why two? It seemed a waste of cloth, the kind of thing Fra Girolamo would scowl at—felt like they were strangling him. "I don't think aiding us is part of his holy orders."

"What does it matter? It gets us inside, Magnus. We are a match for any man, monk or Medici. It was getting through the doors that was worrying me, and here is the solution to our problem." He twirled around, his feet sliding in the too-large sandals, and then gathered up their clothes. Magnus looked longingly at his hose and tunic as they disappeared into the hallway; when Adrian returned, his arms were empty.

"What about our things?" Magnus asked, indicating Adrian's satchel.

"We can pin our papers inside the robe. Leave the rest here." At Magnus's look, he shrugged. "It's not like we have anything important."

"Other than our money?"

"We can always steal more." Adrian waved his hand dismissively. "Hurry and get your papers. We nearly have it, Magnus; I can feel it in my bones."

Sighing, Magnus went back to his own room, trying not to look at the queenly Mary as he went through his satchel. The papers he carried—a letter of introduction, another testifying to his invented place of birth—he slid inside a pouch and pinned under his robe. But here too were his favorite knives, and the misprinted book page he had won at a dice game and was using to teach himself the rudiments of English; here was his favorite linen shirt, worn to an almost-arousing softness. He had other treasures, safely locked away far to the south, but the thought of some idiot monk dulling his knives or scribbling on his page angered him. Fra Girolamo was scheming, Adrian could only think of appeasing Gabriel; what were the odds that he was going to end up with only this shitty habit for his loyalty?

He dug around in the bottom of the bag and found his coin purse, heavy with the money he had won in his bet. With his little knife—oh, such a lovely blade!—he worked the hem of his robe open and began sliding them in.

"Magnus," Adrian called.

One after another, sliding them along the channel of fabric so their little weights were evenly spaced. At least he could use the awkward garment to his advantage. Anyone glancing downward would only see his ankles, not how oddly the skirt of the robe hung.

"Magnus, now," Adrian called, an edge to his voice.

With a last look around the room, he kicked his bag under the bed and left. Adrian stood with Fra Girolamo and two other monks at the end of the hall. One's face was as black as his cloak, the other's tanned to the precise hue of ground wheat; neither were smiling. With his hands clasped humbly before himself and only the torchlight to illuminate them, Adrian might have been one of them, save for the thick waves of hair that fell to his shoulders.

"Come, Magnus," Adrian said. "It is time."

"Yes, my brother. Time to complete your journey," Fra Girolamo said, waving him close. The words made Magnus's stomach ache yet again; still, he placed himself at Adrian's side. Now that he was among them, he saw that the two other monks were both carrying wooden cases, one with a brass lock on it. Money for Lorenzo? He could not see it; it seemed far more likely that Lorenzo would try to bribe the monks.

"We are indebted to you, Fra Girolamo," Adrian said.

"Let us not speak in such base terms. I am merely the Lord's instrument." He led the way out of the convent, past the bright blue fresco now muted by shadows. Magnus and Adrian followed him and the two monks came up behind, their boxes clinking. At the door, a novice saw them out, then slid the bolts loudly into place. As they started to walk, Magnus permitted himself only a brief glance at the monks behind them, their hoods making their expressions unreadable. Beside him, Adrian drew his own hood up, and unwillingly Magnus did the same. As if they too had taken vows; as if they were leaving their former lives behind.

OUTSIDE, the air was cool and damp, a prelude to winter to come. The merchants' stalls were closing for the night, but there were carts offering hot food, and the wine-sellers were doing a brisk trade. Savory odors—cooked sweetbreads and onions, the bite of hot chestnuts—blew over them. There were men in the long black robes and soft hats so common here, walking briskly in conference; a laborer led a mule pulling a small cart, in which a woman and sleeping child sat. An old woman offered them apples; Fra Girolamo paused and spoke with her, gently putting the apples back in her basket, while they waited a polite distance away. In front of a building, stonemasons were packing up their tools for the night: building, everywhere Florence seemed to be building. The jewel of Tuscany. Others spoke of Siena, or Pisa, but there was something about Florence, a kind of emotion all its own. It felt at once of its moment and timeless, outside of the reckoning of man. It did not matter who was Pope, who ruled the distant thrones of France and Spain and the Ottomans. Within Florence there was only Florence.

A trio of young men passed, with two pretty prostitutes between them; they were feeding each other grapes, pressing the fat blood-red orbs to each others' mouths, all laughter and sly whispers and fruit-flecked teeth. One prostitute was especially comely, her thick black hair falling everywhere and her brown throat bared to the cold, her heart beating so vigorously, Magnus fancied he could see it throbbing beneath the swell of her breast ...

His side was punched, hard enough to bruise, and when he turned to Adrian, he was given the look. Pleasure, like sustenance, would have to wait.

Adrian's fear, driving them both.

It took only a few minutes to reach a building seemingly without ornament and yet exuding a sense of power. To see it from afar was to mistake it for a small fortress, drab and unappealing; yet as their little party drew close, Magnus realized it was the most balanced fortress he had ever seen. The word became more right the closer they got: the building was *balanced*, everything exactly in proportion, the stonework resolving into layers of ornamentation that perfectly complemented the solidity of the whole.

They passed an arched loggia to arrive at a pair of heavy wooden doors. Here the two monks crowded in close behind them, barring them from escape—or was it just his fancy? Adrian would say so. But the street was empty; there was plenty of room to stand without their boxes jabbing into his backside. Yet he dared not look at their faces lest he show his own trepidation.

Fra Girolamo knocked and the hollow sound made Magnus's hackles rise. As if it were a call of its own, the knocking made shadows rise out of the loggias on either side. Men, of all ages and standing, their faces strained with hope.

"Are you meeting with Signore Lorenzo?" The nearest one plucked at Fra Girolamo's sleeve; his ear was missing, an old punishment. "Tell him that Benvenuto asks for him; he will know me, little Benvenuto whose father worked the stables at Careggi."

"If you could just bring him my letter," another man said, holding out a paper uncertainly. "He will understand then."

Fra Girolamo waved them off but still they pressed in. Magnus's trepidation became something keener, an animal wariness, but when he nudged Adrian, the latter shook his bowed head once. The monks behind them had turned aside to deal with more petitioners; he had to fight the urge to grab Adrian and simply walk away, walk out of Florence entirely and to hell with everything—

There were footsteps within the palazzo and a small hatch in the door opened. Fra Girolamo passed a note through, then spoke at such a low volume, even Magnus couldn't make out what he was saying. Bolts were opened, the sounds loud in the night; a bar was raised; the doors swung open to reveal bright torchlight and a well-dressed man, his fur-trimmed robe richly gleaming. He waved them inside, waiting while they each scraped the muck from their sandals. As soon as they were all past the threshold, two guards bolted the doors behind them.

"Fra Girolamo," he said warmly, clasping the monk's hand. "I am Niccolò Michelozzi; we have corresponded. We are honored to have you in Florence once more."

They were crowded in a little hall, lit only by two sputtering torches; past the monk and their greeter, however, Magnus could see a courtyard and a walled garden beyond. The air tasted of citrus and perfume and the smells of men: of the discretely pacing guards, of the monks' musty robes pressing close, of a handful of men in animated conversation in the open space. More voices reverberated faintly through the halls. Somewhere, someone was playing an instrument—perhaps a shawm? It seemed yet another voice, one that brought the others into a kind of melody.

"I go where God needs me to be, Messer Michelozzi," Fra Giro-lamo was saying. He gestured to the rest of their party. "Your master sent word he would take the Eucharist this evening, and I have here two companions who I have already written to Lorenzo about. They are to be brought before him after we discuss their circumstances."

Alarmed, Magnus looked at Adrian: why did Fra Girolamo need to discuss them? But Adrian was smiling, smiling, as if all was going as planned. Except they had no plan, they had never had a plan, they had been brought to this moment by fear and the maneuverings of this monk.

"He has already spoken to me of this matter," Niccolò said, bowing low. "Please, follow me."

He led them through the short hall and around the knot of arguing men to enter the courtyard, bathed in moonlight and torchlight both. The men's calculating eyes slid over them; Magnus noted the deep crimson of their robes, the heaviness of the gemstones adorning their necks and hands, and how Fra Girolamo eyed them in turn, his gaze as coldly assessing. No weapons, though; those were the provenance of the guards, of which there were at least four—no, at least six, there were two more in the garden, and probably several more within calling distance.

As their party started to cross the courtyard, they came to an abrupt halt as two boys raced past them, chasing each other around the slender columns ringing the space. All arms and legs, bare-footed, their finely woven shirts and woolen jackets smeared with dirt, calling each other rude names as they swiped and lunged at each other. Niccolò started forward again only to pause as a brown-skinned matron came lumbering down a broad staircase and pushed through them, muttering in a dialect Magnus didn't recognize. The boys hid behind a potted lemon tree, then ran again as the matron caught up to them, leading her back up another, smaller staircase. Niccolò smiled apologetically. "We were all that age once, were we not?" he said, and the two monks behind Magnus laughed and agreed, though Fra Girolamo only smiled in a patronizing way, probably because at that age, he was already scouring himself with his first hairshirt.

Niccolò began walking again, slower now, and Magnus understood that he wanted their gazes to wander, to take in the whole of the spectacle: the airiness of the space, the ornamentation that covered every surface, the red-robed men and the two younger men now strolling down the stairs in pale velvets suitable for princes; the cascade of brown hair and silk shawl from an open window where a pale hand kept delicate time with the shawm, now joined by a lute in a lively tune. If the outside had been an elegant fortress, the inside was a wonder. The columns seemed absurdly slender for the stories above, each banded with friezes; the lights flickering in the windows echoed the stars overhead. The sweetened air became more distinct, several perfumes milling with the potted lemon and laurel trees. But what drew the eye most was the bronze statue centered in the courtyard.

He gazed down at them from beneath a broad-brimmed hat with an oversized feather, his nude body gleaming. Grey-white light from the moon painted his sleek curves, further lit by the flickering torchlight that made the flesh seem to ripple. Smooth enough to touch, to fondle. The light picked out his expression, at once kind and a little sly, his lips about to part, some clever witticism about to be uttered. The ridiculous boots, his thick, wavy hair, the way he balanced atop the head of some monster, as if any soft lad barely out of skirts could kill such a creature—

Magnus nearly stopped as he passed under the bronze gaze, looking at the face, really looking, momentarily forgetting his anxieties. At first, he had thought it merely a resemblance; all but impossible that it could be a likeness, but if it was—oh, it would not be the first time such information had been coyly withheld. He looked pointedly at Adrian, willing him to turn around; and Adrian did, and had the grace to look embarrassed.

"I thought you hadn't been in Tuscany for a century," Magnus whispered as they began ascending a staircase, following the monks and Niccolò, who were halfway up.

"You know perfectly well I have not, since I've been with you for nearly all that time," Adrian retorted, his voice equally soft. "Is it so unusual that there would be someone who looks like me in Florence?"

"You could have just told me," Magnus muttered.

"Told you what? There is nothing to tell!"

"It would in fact be an advantage in this, if you've fucked Lorenzo or one of his circle."

"I have not fucked Lorenzo de' Medici!" Adrian hissed. Their party, already on the landing, to a one paused and looked back at them; both Magnus and Adrian smiled and inclined their heads. When they had turned back to their ascent, however, Adrian continued, "You just want an excuse to be angry at me, because you can't go chasing that whore."

"Yet time and again, the excuses are revealed as truth," Magnus retorted.

"Not this time," Adrian snapped. Again the others turned and looked down at them from the top of the stairs, and again they both smiled and nodded. "Though your suspicions honor me, Magnus; whoever posed for that statue was far more charming than I."

Magnus was prevented from replying by their party, waiting for them before a pair of carved doors. Here on this floor he smelled fresh odors from behind closed doors, several men and women, and heard the thudding of dancing as the players took up another tune; at the far end of the hall he saw two men positioning a small, delicate sculpture in a niche, arguing as one turned it minutely one way and another, the other moving a little oil lamp to catch different angles.

"Lorenzo thought Fra Girolamo might like to see the chapel," Niccolò explained. With a flourish, he opened the doors to a room ablaze in candles and ushered them inside.

"We would of course welcome the friar if he chose to pray among us," he continued; but Magnus only half-heard him, for once again he found himself staring. A fortune in wax lit the room as bright as day, revealing a vast, frescoed procession marching around the chapel, its lines of men streaming in from distant hills dotted with castles, while clouds drifted across a blue sky full of birds. Everywhere he saw movement, men and horses alike, all walking and cantering and waving and twisting, so lifelike he fancied he could hear the clopping of hooves and the voices carrying across the crowd. It stirred old memories of similar journeys, surrounded by his fellows, the heat of the sun on his neck and sweat sticking his clothes to his body and the warm air in his lungs, and he felt the pangs of a grief he had thought long past.

He glanced at Adrian, and for once there was genuine, if mild, interest on his face, a curiosity without caveat or horror. Too, now Magnus saw other details: the fine stonework around the high window, the richly textured ceiling and wainscoting, the red marble altar swathed in blue satin. Even one of the statues of Christ was dressed in red satin trimmed in pearls. What would it be like to live in this place, where everywhere your eye fell was marked by artistry, your very home a temple to the creations of men?

He thought then to ask the monk; surely, he would have some praise for such a room, a divine context for such abundance. But he was surprised to see Fra Girolamo's tightly pursed lips, as if the room were a vast, sour lemon he had been forced to bite.

"I will see your master now," Fra Girolamo said, and the sharpness of his voice seemed to break a spell; the other monks shook themselves, as if brought back from a dream.

Niccolò, however, was unperturbed. "Of course, Fra Girolamo. And your companions?"

"Domenico will come with me. Tomasso can wait here with our friends." He looked at Magnus and Adrian, and Magnus saw it then: the trap, closing. "I can think of no better place for them to bide their time." And with a small, satisfied smile, Fra Girolamo followed Niccolò out, the darker monk trailing behind them.

The other monk settled on a pew near the door, the box on his lap, watching them.

MAGNUS MOVED SLOWLY around the chapel, letting his eyes rest on the details of the frescoes. Here, a man looked out at him with a pained expression—too many miles walked? Here, a bold young man atop a white horse smiled dazzlingly at the world. And there were smaller delights: a falcon with its kill, hounds chasing game in the woods, a particularly attractive pairing of hose—one leg green, one leg crimson; he had always liked how that looked.

On the far side of the chapel, following a similar circuit, Adrian pretended to gaze at the walls, but when he caught Magnus's gaze he arched his eyebrows, clearly irritated. *Well?*

Still Magnus strolled, the eyes of Fra Tomasso following him. The monk was hunched over his box, had surreptitiously reached inside and withdrawn something—probably a knife; the box was a good shape for such. As Magnus drew close to the door, the monk twisted about. "We are to wait here," he said.

Magnus held up his hands. "My apologies. I thought merely to take the air."

"We are waiting for Fra Girolamo," Fra Tomasso snapped. "Respect the hospitality you have been shown."

Magnus bowed. "Of course, Fra Tomasso." He glanced at Adrian, but the latter's back was turned as he pretended to study the little Christ in its red satin gown. Slowly, Magnus began walking once more, his sandals whispering on the polished floor.

Across the room, Adrian suddenly moaned, as if stricken by grief; Fra Tomasso's head jerked towards him; Magnus made his movements noiseless.

"How much longer will it be?" Adrian cried, flinging his arms out. "I cannot bear this waiting!"

"Patience," Fra Tomasso said. The knife was just visible in his sleeve as he angled his head one way and another, trying to see Magnus without turning. Sweat broke out on the monk's body, a crisp, fresh odor atop the incense and musty fabric.

"You do not know how long we have waited, my brother," Adrian ranted, thumping his fist on the pew. "To be so close! What is this delay, why must we linger here?"

Magnus stopped just behind Fra Tomasso and pushed his fangs out. He licked them in turn, first left, then right, savoring the sensation.

"Fra Girolamo had urgent business to discuss with Signore Lorenzo," Fra Tomasso was saying. Again he angled slightly, trying to see Magnus.

"Is not my business urgent? You cannot know how long we have—"

Magnus seized Fra Tomasso around the chest and bit deep into his neck. The monk's arm flew up, stabbing impotently at the air behind himself as Magnus's fangs sank down, down until his teeth rubbed against the skin. Blood welled around the bones and filled his mouth. Fra Tomasso strained and jabbed and then slumped in Magnus's embrace with a sigh, all his will gone as Magnus's spittle took effect. There was a ringing sound as the knife fell to the floor but Magnus barely noticed; the blood, oh, the blood, it was hot and fresh and not a little sweet, it soothed his belly and mind alike, filling him with a clear, wonderful calm. Two, three, and at the fourth mouthful he pulled his fangs free and licked the wounds clean, sealing them with his spit. As he rose, he flicked the box lid up, just a peek inside, then closed it with a sigh.

"That took far too long," Adrian said, kicking the knife aside. "Settle him and let's go."

Magnus only looked at him, licking the last drops from the corner of his mouth. Adrian groaned and put a hand on his hip, halfway between a monk and a scold. "*Now* what is the matter? We are running out of time—"

"We need to leave, Adrian." He spoke slowly, carefully; he had to make him understand. "Look in the box. A hammer and two stakes, and that knife is inlaid with silver." When Adrian's face darkened, he pressed: "We've been brought here deliberately. Two novices will never be remembered. With a dozen men to hand, possibly more? Adrian, *think*. That monk has touched us both; he made us take communion, he knows we won't go out at midday. He's not a fool."

"No, but you are," Adrian retorted. "What does it matter what he thinks? Say he thinks us demons: what do we care? There is nothing in that box that can truly harm us, half the men here are drunk, and if leaving one doughy monk as guard is his measure of us, he's a bigger fool than I thought. In the time you've taken putting that one to sleep, we could have the book already and all of this would be moot." He went to the door of the chapel and eased it open, squinting through the crack.

Gently, Magnus tucked Fra Tomasso's limbs about him so he would stay upright. "I thought this trip was merely to ascertain—"

Adrian silenced him with a hiss, and with a grimace Magnus followed him out into the hallway. Here they stood, still and alert, each sensing: the stillness of the shadows beyond the glow of the single hanging lamp, the remains of supper in the air, the dancing party deeper in the building, the guards pacing in the courtyard below. At the far end of the hall was an open door, bright with candlelight and smelling of men and wine, and a dark staircase leading tantalizingly down as well as up. Adrian began walking boldly toward the staircase and Magnus caught his arm, pointing at the open door and giving Adrian a look of his own: what had happened to *at any price save suspicion*? They had no excuses worked out, no retreat planned—and he could not shake the feeling that this too was somehow part of the monk's plotting, though he could not fathom why.

For a moment, they glared at each other; and then there was a cry from the open door and the sound of a chair scraping. Magnus shoved Adrian back in the chapel just as a young man, his handsome face flushed, stepped out into the hall. "More wine!" he bellowed, stamping his foot as if in emphasis, and went back inside. His return was met with cheers and a call about betting; cards or dice, Magnus surmised. From the sounds, there were at least three others in the room, possibly more.

"Gambling at the end of the hall, dancing across the way, and who knows how many more above and below," Magnus whispered. "And the book could be anywhere."

"Then the sooner we look for it, the sooner we will find it," Adrian whispered back.

There was an edge to his voice now that Magnus recognized, a tension in his jaw: there would be no swaying him save with violence. From the end of the hall came the sound of heavy footsteps descending, and he laid a hand on Adrian's shoulder. "Wait here," he said.

He stepped out of the chapel, arranging his face so as to look abashed, and moved halfway down the hall, keeping in the shadows. An older man in a frayed woolen tunic, stooped with age, was descending with a jug of wine in his arms, squinting to make out the steps; he paused as he caught sight of Magnus beckoning to him, then kept descending. Clearly, novices in ill-fitting robes were not that uncommon a sight in the house of Lorenzo de' Medici. His short hair was a thinning grey, his hands gnarled from work. At the last riser, he angled his body, hiding the jug from view, and moved swiftly past the open door to Magnus.

"My brother, forgive me," Magnus murmured, keeping his voice low. "Only, Fra Girolamo asked me to fetch a book for him to consult with Signore Lorenzo, and like a fool, I left without asking where the books are kept. To go back now and ask for directions, I do not want the friar to lose face …"

At his words, the old man's face softened. "The whole damn place is full of books," he said. "But most are in the library. Very top of the stairs, turn left. The door has an amulet over it."

Magnus grinned, his relief unfeigned, and bowed again. "Thank you, my brother. Thank you."

"You can thank me by blessing me," the old man replied, looking back at the open door. "They're kind enough when sober, but when they're in their cups? Animals, the lot. They will have wanted one of the women to come—! Like sending a rabbit into a den of wolves."

Magnus's heart sank. Bless him? All his memories of such seemed to vanish from his mind. "I—I have not yet taken my vows."

"Surely, you can bless a man, though." The man looked at him keenly, though whether from suspicion or just trying to see in the gloomy hall, Magnus wasn't sure. "I am but a poor man trying to survive, yet you cannot say a kind word for me?"

With a tight smile, Magnus made the sign of the cross over the man. Right to left, or left to right? He guessed, and hoped he had guessed correctly. "Dominus vobiscum," he said, trying to sound authoritative. Was there more to it? Why hadn't he paid more attention before this?

"Thank you, brother," the old man said, but the keen look had not left his face. He went back to the open door, holding the wine before him like an offering; a chorus of cheers and boos alike met him, only to be smothered to a rumbling when the door was shut.

Adrian came out of the chapel. "Well?"

"Library is at the top of the stairs, turn left, the door with the amulet—"

Before he had finished speaking, Adrian was down the hall and up the stairs, a dark blur climbing swiftly and silently, the white robe flashing beneath the black cloak. Magnus followed more cautiously; what if they were seen? But Adrian's luck held and he vanished into the shadows above.

On the third floor, the odors changed: now there were more women, children, smells of milk and food. From an open window came the lute again, now accompanying a woman's voice

Non val acqua al mio gran foco,
che per pianto non si amorza
anzi ognhor più se rinforza

quanto più con quel mi sfoco

And still Magnus could not stop looking. Even here, far from public scrutiny, every piece of wood was deeply carved, the tiled floors patterned, the ceilings decorated. Small sculptures dotted the corners, and painted panels hung between the ornate cornices. It was almost too much; so much detail, it was starting to make his head hurt.

All his time with Adrian, traveling to Gotland, to the estates and villas of the other dangenes as emissaries, and not a one of them came anywhere near this display. Il Magnifico indeed. There was something in that discrepancy, he knew, something that had meaning for their own circumstance; he would have to ask Adrian about it, he would have to find the words to ask with.

And he had dawdled long enough. He hurried up the stairs to the fourth floor, past rooms with sleeping bodies, the thick odors of a kitchen. The library door stood open, marked by a large, ornate amulet tacked above it as the old man had described and smelling of leather and wax. This, at least, was familiar—he had never met a wealthy man who didn't fancy himself an alchemist, as if wealth was a fever that could only be cured by more wealth. But then Magnus stepped into the room and all his muddled worries and musings vanished, replaced by a cold weight of horror.

Here was the Medici library: books, so many books, filling every wall and three separate tables. There was easily more than a hundred volumes, perhaps two? Three? He had never seen so many books in a house before. As he entered the room, he nearly tripped over an open crate, filled with quires waiting for binding. More were stacked on one of the tables, surrounded by two sewing frames, pots of glue and spools of thread, and a neat pyramid of fresh wax tapers.

"Shit," he said aloud.

Adrian had lit a single candle, balanced precariously on the window sill, and was pulling books off the shelves one by one, peeking inside before shoving it back and grabbing the next. His face was damp with sweat: not good. As Magnus closed the door, he pulled another off the shelf and glanced at the text. "Had a lovely stroll, did we?" he snapped, his voice high with tension. "A beautiful night for such; why not take another turn?"

Magnus just looked at him. Downstairs the music rose up again, a singalong now, several voices chorusing in time with the lute

Passando per una rezolla
De questa terra de questa terra
Li passa lo mio amore
Li passa lo mio amore

"Well? What are you waiting for?" Adrian shoved the book back, punching the leather spine.

"Adrian," Magnus said gently. "There isn't enough time."

Adrian ignored him, his fingers scrabbling to pull out the next book, grunting a little as he pulled two free at once.

"Adrian," he said again, moving closer to him, watching as Adrian pulled out a small, slim volume. The surrounding books fell over; he struggled to push the little book back until Magnus leaned over him and held the space open. "We are being introduced tonight," he continued patiently. "We can ask for a tour, get a sense of the house as a whole, confirm the book is indeed here. Why throw away that opportunity? Resort to outright theft now and it will be all over the city by daybreak—exactly what we were supposed to avoid."

"We will avoid it by finding the book and getting away swiftly," Adrian retorted. "You know what their language looks like—"

"—and it will take too long," Magnus finished. "There are too many books, and who's to say it's even here? That servant said there were books everywhere. For all we know, he could be using it to prop up a table."

Adrian didn't respond, only jerked another book off the shelf.

"I have a rough count of the guards now, and the garden walls will be easy to scale." When Adrian didn't respond he pressed: "We can come back tomorrow night, the night after, as many nights as it takes."

"Tomorrow, tomorrow, tomorrow," Adrian said, rounding on him. "And what if we can't, Magnus? What if tomorrow is too late? This may be our only chance." His voice was rising into a frantic whine; when Magnus simply looked at him he slapped Magnus, so hard that lights flashed in Magnus's vision. "What are you waiting for? I am ordering you to find it!"

Still Magnus just looked at him, keeping his burning face expressionless. Decades since Adrian had last raised his hand to him. Another slap, and another, the blows driving Magnus back against a table. Decades, but he hadn't forgotten, he knew better than to try and dodge or block them and instead gripped the edge of the table until the wood cracked beneath his fingers.

"We are going to find it," Adrian said, his voice loud in the room. "We are going to find it and we are going to bring it to him and we are going to *appease* him, do you understand, can you get that through your thick skull? That is what will happen, even if I have to tear this palazzo apart and everyone in it."

The burning pain was already fading as his body healed; still Magnus felt himself bruised, marked. His jaw throbbed as he managed, "You know as well as I no book will appease him. It's just a game, a ploy to see what we'll do."

Another blow, backhanded; Magnus felt a tooth loosen. "You would explain *Gabriel* to *me?*" Adrian was spitting the words out now, his face so contorted, he seemed another person entirely. "You think a few months in his cellars is the limit of him? Or are you so eager to be his pet? You should have said something, Magnus; I would gladly have exchanged—"

But he broke off abruptly, staring. Magnus was trying to absorb Adrian's fury, to transmute it into calm as he used to, but he could not stop his eyes welling. A year since Gotland and it might as well have been yesterday.

"Of course I cannot know him as you do. I will *never* know him as you do." He took a shuddering breath. "But I know *you*. I know he wants you afraid and jumping at his every whim, and I know you are better than—"

He broke off, trying to steady his voice. Still Adrian stared at him, his own eyes reddened and welling, saying nothing.

"I know you are better than that," he ground out. "I know you can *be* better than that. Only, you won't listen; you won't ever fucking *listen*." His breath was tight now, so tight. "Do you truly think I wouldn't have taken your place? Do you truly believe I would ever, *ever* have let him touch you, if you hadn't stepped forward? I told you then I was not worth it. *I was not worth it.* But you won't ever *listen*—"

Adrian lurched forward and laid a hand on his chest. "No," he whispered. "No. Don't ever say that, Magnus. That's not ... I mean, I didn't ..." He bowed his head. "Shit," he whispered.

A silence fell over the room. Even the music below had stopped; the hush felt unearthly. The moment stretched between them as the last of the fury ebbed from Adrian's features, replaced by a sorrow that hurt Magnus to see. Yet he held his tongue, feeling the cool pressure of that single point of contact between them, his tooth tightening back in its socket, the last of the pains fading as if they had never been.

"Magnus," Adrian finally murmured. "Magnus, I'm—"

But he broke off at the sound of footsteps in the hall. Two, possibly three men, their steps heavy and certain. The hand fell away and they both wiped roughly at their faces. Adrian took a deep, shaky breath, and another; Magnus rolled his shoulders. He indicated the lone window, but Adrian shook his head.

"The die has been cast," he said, his voice almost normal.

If the men were startled to find two red-eyed novices, one slight and dark, one too tall and sickly pale, standing in a nearly lightless room amidst a mess of spilled glue, they did not show it. Two were armed, and Magnus silently added them to the guard tally; the third was the old man who had carried the wine, now holding a large candelabra and sporting a dark stain down his front.

"If you please," he said with a slight bow. "Signore Lorenzo will see you now."

Adrian turned to go, but Magnus caught his arm, stilling him. "Thank you, but I have not found the book I was sent for," he said. "We'll be there in a moment."

But the old man only smiled; he glanced at one of the guards, who grinned at him, clearly sharing a joke.

"The book you seek is not here, *brother*," the old man said. "Signore Lorenzo says to tell you that if you want it, you will have to come and get it."

4

THE BEDROOM DOOR had been opened by none other than Fra Girolamo, looking even more sour; he waved them in with a twisting of his lips that could in no way be construed as a smile. The room was large and pleasant, bright with candlelight and lamplight both, though smelling of sickness and smoke alike. The walls were dotted with canvases and mosaics; there were busts over the doors and small sculptures in the corners, so that it seemed to Magnus that a dozen pairs of lifeless eyes watched their every move. A fire burned low in the hearth and there was a broad table piled with even more books. He wanted to say to Adrian, *See? What did I tell you?* But there would be time for such recriminations later.

The centerpiece of the room was a vast, carved bed, its layers of creamy curtains pinned back, and on the bed lay a man. He was dressed like any fellow from the street, in a yellowing shirt and a simple black tunic, yet he exuded an authority that eclipsed even Fra Girolamo's coiled fervor. His dark hair was threaded with grey, his wan, tired face as handsome as a bulldog's; yet Magnus felt drawn to him, had a sudden urge to sit down and explain all to Lorenzo de' Medici.

Beside him was Fra Domenico, putting away a vial, and another servant, tall and lumpish with muscle, gazing at everything and nothing. Fra Girolamo moved around the bed to stand by Lorenzo; behind Magnus and Adrian, the guards crowded into the doorway. If nothing else, it was familiar territory: boxed in by men. Not enough to truly threaten them; still, Magnus didn't fancy the violence it would take to break out of the room and escape.

From beneath the layers of white bedcovers one of Lorenzo's bare legs emerged, wrapped in cloths. Here, then, was the source of the sickroom smell, of a body confined. Adrian had told Magnus of some kind of illness among the Medici, an inherited gout or its like. Even Lorenzo il Magnifico, it seemed, was not exempt from such frailties.

"As per your request, which was passed to every brother from here to the sea," Fra Girolamo said, pronouncing the words like they were a curse. "Two men such as you described: unusual in their habits and imbalanced in their humors, seeking a book in your possession. Delivered with no identification and no cause to be noticed."

Magnus bit back his exclamation; beside him, Adrian began sniggering, then openly laughing. To Magnus's astonishment, Lorenzo began to smile as well. How far in advance had he been plotting—and what, or who, had alerted him to do so? He felt blindsided; instinctively he inhaled, but no, there was no army awaiting them without, no mob filling the courtyard. At once all the monk's little gestures, his odd turns of phrase, fell into a much different pattern. The resignation he had shown outside the gate was not that of facing an annoying petitioner, but of being the one stuck delivering the goods.

"You have done well, Fra Girolamo," Lorenzo said. "Better than well. I am grateful to the order for their assistance in this matter. It will not be forgotten."

Adrian was still cackling away. Magnus only watched, noting

every twitch of the men's faces, how the guards continued blocking the door, his own body tense with anticipation.

"We are not grateful," Fra Girolamo snapped. "We are not your servants, Lorenzo de' Medici. I have completed this task because my predecessor at San Marco gave you his word, but I tell you now: your money can buy much, but it no longer buys the souls of my brothers for your unholy dealings. The host this morning sickened these so-called men as I have never seen, and Tommaso is now marked by their foul touch. At best they are possessed; at worst they are demons in disguise. Yet you will not let us—silence, creature!" he barked, glaring at Adrian, who was still tittering.

"Forgive him, signori," Magnus said carefully, inclining his head. "It has been some time since we had cause to laugh."

Adrian swallowed. "Unbalanced humors," he gasped, and burst into fresh giggles.

"As I was saying"—Fra Girolamo turned his back deliberately to them—"they may be demons made flesh, yet you will not let us perform a simple exorcism or otherwise test their faith. At the very least, they should be driven from the city—"

"Yes, yes." Lorenzo looked at the burly servant, who promptly went to a bowl on a nearby table; carefully he wrung out a rag, then replaced one of the cloths on Lorenzo's leg. Magnus glimpsed an obscenely swollen ankle that just as quickly vanished under its fresh compress. A new smell rose up, something herbal that burned his nostrils. Lorenzo sighed deeply and his body relaxed, as if released from some stricture. "It will be fine, Fra Girolamo."

"Is that the sum of your response?" Fra Girolamo demanded, nearly hissing out the words. "Your wealth has made you contemptuous, Signore Lorenzo, contemptuous to the point of cruelty. Is it not enough that people starve in the street while you sit here in your palace? That they cry out for help and you give them nothing but debauchery and spectacle? Must you sacrifice their souls as well for your vainglory?"

Lorenzo looked up at the monk then, all softness gone. Magnus readied himself; beside him, Adrian finally quieted. A silence fell over the room as the two men stared at each other, Lorenzo's face expressionless, Fra Girolamo's reddening with anger.

"We have business, these men and I," Lorenzo finally said. "Family business that does not concern you. And even if we did not"—his voice raised as Fra Girolamo tried to speak—"even if we did not, Fra Girolamo, they are *my* guests in *my* home, and they will be shown the hospitality of the Medici."

"And what of Tommaso? He too is a guest, one who has been obscenely violated in *your* home. I demand—"

Lorenzo raised his hand, and the silence fell once more, weighted and ominous. He waited, letting the moment stretch until Fra Girolamo was almost snarling; only then did he speak. "We apologize for the insult, Fra Girolamo, and rest assured we will investigate the matter thoroughly. And of course Fra Tommaso will be cared for at my expense. I'm sure you will want to take him back to the convent now."

Fra Girolamo's mouth opened and shut, like a fish's. The burly servant took a step closer to him; the old man went to the door and swung it open with a bow.

Clearly furious, the monk slowly walked around the bed, his glowering stare sweeping from Lorenzo to Magnus and Adrian in turn. He nodded at Fra Domenico, who gathered up the wooden box and made to leave, but suddenly Fra Girolamo lunged for the box and seized a flask. In one smooth motion he whirled about, uncorked the flask, and with a snap of his wrist flung its contents at Magnus and Adrian.

Water splashed on Magnus's face and the front of his robe. Fra Girolamo's face was a mixture of astonishment and anger; his second looked distinctly nervous. But the guards had not changed their stance, and the old man was smirking.

"A pity to waste your water, Fra Girolamo," Adrian said, dabbing his face with his sleeve. "But perhaps your concerns can now be laid to rest?"

"Never, fiend," the monk spat. "I do not know what kind of abomination you represent, but I will not rest—"

"That is enough," Lorenzo barked. He was struggling to sit upright, but his voice rang with authority; Magnus had the sense of two great wills clashing, like waves crashing into each other. "Tend to your sphere, Fra Girolamo, and I will tend to mine."

He gave a sharp nod to the burly servant, who advanced on the two monks, his hand held out toward the door. Fra Girolamo gave Lorenzo one last, dark look; and then his face smoothed out. "Signore Lorenzo is wiser than I first understood," he said. "I will follow his advice, though may he forgive me if I forget this meeting ever took place." He bowed, so low his hood fell over his head. Flipping it back impatiently, he stormed from the room, his second close at his heels.

Lorenzo waved the old man close and whispered to him, so softly even Magnus couldn't hear what he was saying; and then the old man ushered the burly servant and the guards out, following them and closing the door. The guards, Magnus knew, had not gone far, but they were effectively alone. The silence fell once more as Lorenzo stared at them, an almost unearthly hush punctuated only by the crackle of the fireplace.

"You are not what I expected," Lorenzo finally said.

"Nor are you, Signore Lorenzo," Adrian replied at once, a smile tugging at his lips again.

"My grandfather told me of men with the faces of serpents." He leaned back against the pillows with a sigh. "I thought he was trying to frighten me—was he?"

"There are but a few of us who would fit such a description." Adrian spread his arms and turned around. "The rest of us are as like men as brothers are to brothers."

"You are also remarkably like our David below. Perhaps you had a relation who was known to Donato? Donato Bardi? He was the sculptor."

At the name Adrian's eyes widened; he looked at Magnus,

visibly chagrined. *That summer in Rome*, he mouthed. Magnus only sniffed.

"Brothers to brothers indeed," Lorenzo continued, though Magnus knew he hadn't missed their exchange. "It has been a long time since such beauty presented itself in my chambers ..." He trailed off, then shook himself. "But you have the advantage of me, Messers, and that will not do in my own house. You know my name, but I do not know yours."

At that Adrian laughed. "And I apologize for being remiss, Signore Lorenzo. I am Adrian, and this is Magnus, my second."

"No family name?"

"None that you would recognize."

"Hmph. I used to advocate for self-made men. Lately, however?" He smiled a little; sadly, it seemed to Magnus. "It can be a difficult thing, to be a father. It would be more so if I did not have the comfort of knowing my name will continue."

Adrian shrugged, but Magnus could see the sentiment rankled. "As sons are so rarely privy to their father's innermost thoughts, Signore Lorenzo, I will bow to your experience."

"So, what will you give me for the book?"

The question, asked in the same tone, startled Adrian; and then he laughed. "We are so quick to sell? I thought you would want to debate the matter."

"If you were men, certainly. We would eat and drink and speak of many things, and in good time arrive at an exchange satisfying to us both." Lorenzo waved his hand at them. "But by your own admission, you are not men. My grandfather said you live by the most perverse of sustenance, and that money, possessions, these have no meaning for you; but Cosimo also believed that what a man does value is the key to his character—the seed of his truer nature. So, tell me, Messer Adrian, what do creatures such as yourself value?"

Magnus glanced at Adrian, then did a double take. Adrian's lips were slightly parted; he knew that look. It was interest, genuine interest in the sickly man before them.

"All that you have said is true, Signore Lorenzo," Adrian said slowly. "We are as you describe; in fact, we are here merely on a whim. The book is unfamiliar to us, and there is little in the world that we are not familiar with. I suppose you could say we value novelty above all."

"You have gone through some straits for novelty," Lorenzo remarked. "Traveling with a friar of Savonarola's piety, scouting the road from Bologna for competitors? This whole business of reclaiming a family heirloom? Though I suppose I should be grateful, Messers, that you did not go so far as to slander me. If you were to put it about that my family steals from churches, I would be forced to reply."

The last was delivered with firmness. Again that iron will; Magnus smiled a little. No matter his health, there was no question who was king of this castle—and perhaps the whole of the city around him. "We would not think to insult you in such fashion, Signore Lorenzo," he said.

There was a knock on the door, and at Lorenzo's call the elderly servant entered, carrying a book in his arms. He handed it to Lorenzo and withdrew again with a bow; Magnus glimpsed a guard just outside the door. They could be inside in a heartbeat.

"Well, Messers." Lorenzo spread the book open on his lap, thumbing through the worn vellum pages. "Here is the book in question. Now what can you offer me—"

But Adrian was shaking his head. "Do not dissemble so, Signore Lorenzo. It suits you ill. That is not the book we seek."

The pages stopped turning; the gaze that looked up through the loose dark hair was sly. "And how would you know that?"

"Because that book is in Greek." Adrian moved close to the bed; he reached out and slid his forefinger across the vellum, stroking the page. "A lovely volume, I will admit; were I a collector, I would pay a pretty price for such a tome. But what we seek is in a very different language."

Lorenzo's eyes flicked down to that slow, sliding finger, watching it for a heartbeat with parted lips. "Not too different," he said. "There is more than a little Greek in it, I think, and other words that resemble texts found in the east. Some phrases, I will admit, have remained opaque to us; but we have managed to translate quite a few. The title, for instance. Taiart Gal—the Second Coming."

The effect of his words on Adrian was profound. For the first time in—how long? He could not remember the last time— Magnus saw utter shock appear on Adrian's face. He jerked backward, holding his hand to his chest as if burned. "What did you say the book was called?" he said huskily.

"Taiart Gal." Smoothly Lorenzo closed the sham book and laid it aside. "It seems we have cause to bargain after all, Messers."

Adrian turned abruptly and walked to the fire, staring at the smoldering flames as if within them was some answer desperately sought. Magnus saw he had gone pale, pale and trembling, but he dared not question him with Lorenzo present. Instead, he asked, "May we see the real book, Signore Lorenzo?"

In response, the man turned stiffly in bed, reaching around to the ornately carved headboard behind him. He pressed the wood and a small door opened; with some care he prised forth a slim, leather-bound codex. Its edges were crumbling with age, its pages yellowed and ragged, but when he opened it the text was crisp. He turned it toward Magnus, keeping it on his lap.

Magnus leaned over to study it—and then all became terribly clear. Though he could barely read the language—he had only learned a few words, none of them good ones—he knew the shape of it. Sereidenikè. But he did not have to see more than that first page, which showed a crude drawing of a winged serpent, to remember what *Taiart Gal* meant.

Not the *Second Coming*; a better translation was the *Great*

Return. A prophecy about the return of the Nagac, the great serpent which had created the sereidees millennia before. No one had seemed to think it more than a story, or even think of it at all. Until now.

"May I?" he asked, gesturing to the pages. Lorenzo nodded.

Page after page, there was nothing but text, the words in smooth, unbroken lines. Until another image: this of many circles and overlapping circular lines, with little figures and symbols notated throughout; in the center swirled another serpent, coiled to touch its own tail. A map of the heavens. There had been astronomers in Gotland, the first time Magnus could remember such, working with the feverish panic typical of Gabriel's clutch of human servants, for whom both success and failure could be equally terrifying.

Magnus looked again at Adrian, still staring at the fire. Gabriel, searching for *this* book, not wanting the other families to know. The frantic astronomers scurrying to and fro, clutching astrolabes and rolls of parchment. *At any price save suspicion.* He and Adrian had speculated on the way to Florence, had decided the book was either yet another alchemical treatise or a history with useful gossip. But this was something else, something either utterly foolish or utterly portentous, and Gabriel was rarely foolish.

Lorenzo too was watching Adrian, watching the shuddering body and the straining fist resting against the mantelpiece. "Am I right in assuming that this is not the book you were expecting?"

"Not exactly," Magnus said, trying to think. What should they do, what could they do? "May I ask how you came by it?"

"My grandfather was a great collector of books." Lorenzo's gaze softened. "Cosimo believed there was tremendous wisdom to be found in neglected writings, and it was one of our duties as citizens to bring that wisdom to Florence. He sent agents far and wide to buy whatever they thought might benefit our collection. He corresponded with scholars, princes, alchemists, always looking for guidance, for knowledge." He blinked, then looked down at the codex in his lap. "But this book came to him."

Adrian's head turned slightly, listening.

"It was given as surety for a loan—a loan for whom, he never knew. All was conducted through an intermediary who subsequently vanished. Its age and language intrigued Cosimo, and he invited several scholars to examine it, but while they could parse a few phrases, it was never enough to grasp the full meaning. One night, he had a friend to supper, an alchemist, and he thought to show off his curiosity—and the alchemist knew it at once." Lorenzo looked at Magnus, his gaze keen once more. "The alchemist said it was fate that had brought this book to Cosimo de' Medici, for it was a gift from God to mankind: the means to survive a future cataclysm, when the very serpent of Eden returned to torment man once more."

"Shit," Magnus muttered. At Lorenzo's arched eyebrow he shook his head. "My apologies. Please, continue."

"Such a gift could not be entrusted to just any man, the alchemist explained. There were agents of the devil who would seek the book, perhaps in the guise of men, perhaps in their true serpentine form. It would take great strength of will to keep the book from them, because they would offer many temptations: wealth, knowledge, and ... health."

The last was pronounced with such heaviness that Adrian turned around completely, comprehension dawning on his face. Lorenzo peeled back the layers of cloth on his leg, revealing a reddened limb so swollen as to seem distended. *Gout, or something like*, Adrian had said. But the name of the affliction did not matter; the pain on Lorenzo's face told them all they needed to know.

"Cosimo offered the book to the alchemist," Lorenzo continued, his voice a pained whisper. "But the alchemist refused. He had been born with a curved spine, you see; he did not trust himself to resist. He was right about my grandfather, though. I do not know if Cosimo was ever tempted, but he kept the book close, as did my father after him." He looked from Magnus to Adrian, his gaze hollow. "But I am not the men they were, Messers, and my son, may he forgive me, is not the man I am. I know death approaches, I sense it like—like a shadow, on the horizon. I know this is God's will, I pray every day to be made strong enough to bear it. But—" He paused, steadying the tremor in his voice. "But Piero is not yet ready to take my place; Piero may *never* be ready."

And then Lorenzo de' Medici wept, the drying cloths crumpled in his hands, his swollen, red leg before him like a terrible admonition, as terrible as the codex that lay on the coverlet.

THEY HAD CALLED for wine for Lorenzo, and the burly servant returned with a fresh bowl of the herbal water and replaced the cloths on his master's leg; in that time, Magnus drew Adrian close to the fireplace again. "What do we do?" he asked quietly.

"I—I don't know," Adrian whispered. His gaze was as hollow as Lorenzo's had been. "I don't know, Magnus."

"How bad could it be, if he gets this book? What might he do with it?"

"I don't know!" His face was almost pallid in the firelight. "I don't remember him scheming like this before. The secrecy, the wording of his letter? It felt odd, but I thought he was just testing us."

Magnus glanced over his shoulder at Lorenzo, calmer now, holding the book close to his face to study the words. "Do you know what the prophecy says?"

Adrian pressed a hand over his eyes. "That ... that the serpent will come as it had before. A reckoning, of what was done with its blood. Its progeny called to judgment. A sacrifice. I can't remember what else."

"There is a map of the heavens in the book." He lowered his voice further. "Perhaps a portent, or a time for the actual event?

Either way, I'm guessing an astronomer could interpret it in some manner. How could Gabriel use that information?"

Adrian shuddered at his words. "I don't know," he whispered. "There are some who believe that story ... believe it fervently ... I never thought he did, but perhaps he could use it against them? Or perhaps he's come to believe it as well? It sounds impossible, but any rational man would say the same of us." His eyes were welling. "If—if it were *true* ... if a source of pure blood fell from the heavens, and he seized it for himself ..."

His voice broke. Magnus saw the gleam of tears on his dark lashes, the defeat that seemed to make his whole body wilt. The firelight painting his ghastly face yellow. *A prize for an emperor,* Gabriel had once said, seizing Adrian's jaw and turning his face one way and another. *But what is an emperor to one such as I? All prizes are mine for the taking.*

They could not go back to Gotland, ever.

He went back to Lorenzo's bedside; something in his face made Lorenzo dismiss the burly servant once more. Magnus gestured to the foot of the bed, and at Lorenzo's nod he settled himself there, careful to keep from brushing against the swollen limb.

"Tell me of what ails you," he said.

Lorenzo hesitated. "They say it is gout, though it seems a kind peculiar to my family. Cosimo and Piero, my father, both had it. And I fear—I fear our lives are getting successively shorter. Piero did not make Cosimo's years, and I feel in my bones I will not make his. I fear for my children," he added softly. "Though my sisters, thanks be to God, seem to have been spared. Perhaps my daughters will be as well." He was silent for a moment, then smiled slyly at Magnus, an echo of the man who had stared down Fra Girolamo only a short time before. "There are some in this city who say the Medici are being punished for our sins, Messer Magnus. If that's true, who better than an agent of the devil to grant me some relief?"

Magnus found himself smiling back. Again he had an urge to confess all to Lorenzo, to explain about Gabriel and his race, the prophecy and its implications. Gabriel thought men no more than ants to his greatness, but like all his kind he had created around himself a chorus of underlings that echoed his sentiments. An intelligent, canny man, distanced from the fear and absurdity of Gotland? He might cut through their problems in a way Magnus or Adrian could not. But such a confession, were it traced back to Magnus, would bring them back to that hell with no escape.

Instead, he looked back at Adrian: *Well?* Adrian hesitated, then reluctantly tapped his mouth and nodded at Lorenzo. An honest offer, then.

"Would that it were so simple, Signore Lorenzo." Magnus spread his hands. "What the alchemist said is true: we have some ability to heal the sick. Were you thrown from a horse, or beaten badly, we could restore you to yourself. But we cannot influence an inherited illness. We can ease your pain; we can help you to feel better for some days. But we cannot cure you. And for that I am truly sorry," he added. For he was.

For a brief moment, Lorenzo's face crumpled in disappointment; and then it smoothed out, as if they had merely been discussing the weather. "What do you mean by *ease it*?" he asked. There was a faint tremor in his voice, testament to all his smothered anguish.

Again Magnus glanced at Adrian before speaking, taking the latter's tense silence as tacit approval. "If you drink our blood, it will ease your pain for a time. How long I cannot say; it affects every man differently. But we can give you some now and leave you more. It will keep for a few days in a corked bottle underground."

He heard Adrian's soft inhale behind him, felt a frisson of anxiety even as he spoke. They were not supposed to barter with their blood or explain its limitations. A great deal of Gabriel's empire was founded on the misapprehension that their blood was a miracle without conditions—or so Gabriel believed. In Magnus's experience, most men knew that miracles always came with caveats, and Lorenzo de' Medici would be no exception.

"And you offer this in exchange for the book?" Lorenzo asked. "A foul medicine that may or may not work?"

Magnus shook his head. "No, Signore Lorenzo. I am offering you a medicine that may or may not work, in exchange for you burning the book."

His words were met with a resounding silence. Lorenzo gaped at him, then looked past him to Adrian. "Is this what you want?"

Adrian shook himself at Lorenzo's words, then, unwillingly, drew close again. His eyes danced everywhere, alighting on everything save the book. "In all honesty, Signore Lorenzo? I do not trust myself in this. But—" He took a breath. "But I trust in my second."

The words their own kind of warmth; Magnus found himself smiling in return. Adrian was almost shy as he nodded, the briefest approval, and withdrew to a corner.

"I have done many things in my life," Lorenzo said heavily, "but I have never destroyed a book."

"But you know the power they can contain," Magnus replied. "On paper can be written such knowledge, such secrets, as can undo kingdoms ... or enact cataclysms." *Or fuel Gabriel's ambitions*, he thought. "May I ask if copies have been made?"

"No copies," Lorenzo said—but he spoke too quickly, and his heartbeat stuttered, and Magnus's own heart sank in response. Of course a man such as Lorenzo would have made a copy, perhaps several copies. Copies were security; copies were second chances. But burning the one, at least, might buy them a little time— enough to get Adrian someplace remote, someplace where they could reason matters through.

Aloud he said, "So, do we have a bargain?"

But Lorenzo was looking from him to Adrian; slowly, almost regretfully, he shook his head. "You should not make demands when you are in straits, Messer Magnus," he said. "You came here to steal a book for your so-called father, and then you found it was not what you expected—that you had been used. Instead, you think, *Let Lorenzo destroy it, and then I can look my father in the eye and say,* It was not our doing. But you are asking me to destroy a legacy for men everywhere. How could I look my own sons in the eye and say I took the word of an unholy creature and destroyed a book I had not even read?"

Magnus stared at him, astonished; before he could think of a reply, Lorenzo held up his hand.

"Here is my bargain. We will try this medicine of yours, and see if it affects me. If I feel relief, your master will read the book to me. I know enough of the language that I will know if he tries to invent meanings, so let us not even bother with that ploy. Once I know what it says, I will make my decision about whether or not to destroy it."

Still Magnus was staring. "What if we just take it?" he blurted out.

Lorenzo shrugged. "Then you will have no excuse not to deliver it. Which, frankly, does not seem like it will be good for either of you." He looked at Adrian, and the naked interest in his gaze made Magnus's stomach lurch. "What does our David say?"

"Signore Lorenzo, do you understand what we truly are?" Magnus demanded. "You cannot dictate terms—"

"It's all right," Adrian said from the corner. When Magnus turned, startled, he was smiling. "It's all right, Magnus. He has a right to know what he's being asked to do." He bowed to the bed. "It would be my pleasure to read to you, Signore Lorenzo. Are we agreed?"

Lorenzo looked at him, letting his gaze sweep from Adrian's head to his feet and back again. "Oh, I very much agree," he agreed softly. "And the medicine?"

"It is better coming from me, as you instinctively understood." Adrian drew close once more, laying his hand on Magnus's shoulder. "Wait outside, Magnus."

Magnus looked at him, feeling sick, trying to read Adrian's expression. "I—I didn't mean ..." His voice a whisper; Lorenzo was watching them closely.

"I know," Adrian said, gently rubbing his shoulder. "It's all right, Magnus. I am *choosing* this. I'm choosing this because you're *right*." He flashed him a warmer smile then: open, reassuring. "Though this is the only time you will get me to admit it."

"Your concern is a credit to you both," Lorenzo said, his voice tight with pain. He waved at the drying compresses. "But I am no threat to your master, Messer Magnus, as you can see. Only, it's been so long since true beauty graced me with its presence ..."

Slowly Adrian stepped out of the too-big sandals. He drew off the black hood with a flourish, and let the cloak flutter to the floor; he peeled off the outer layers of white, then slowly unknotted the cincture and let it slither atop the piled fabrics. At last he slid the tunic up, up, inexorably rising past thighs and hips until at last he stood naked before Lorenzo. The firelight dappled his body as he turned one way and another: a statue among so many, come to life.

"Thank you," Lorenzo breathed. "Thank you." His voice almost fervent.

"Do not thank me yet, Signore Lorenzo," Adrian replied. "We have only just begun." He nodded at Magnus, then mouthed, *Stay close.*

Magnus rose and bowed, but he took his time leaving, keeping his gaze on Adrian. The first sign of any hesitation, any doubt or fear, and he would carry him off—

Adrian took up a wineglass and poured a little in, then extended his fangs. The hiss from Lorenzo, equal parts fear and wonder as Adrian dragged a single sharp tooth down his wrist and let the blood well, then dribble into the wine. Every drop audible. *Mio amore*, Lorenzo whispered. Adrian leaned over and held the cup to the lips of Lorenzo de' Medici, and that was enough; Magnus shut the door on them both.

IN THE HALL, Magnus nodded at the guards, who simply looked at him. Hard men, their faces and hands scarred; they weren't simply for show. *He is like a king, though he is only a citizen,* Adrian had said. Such precarity, and with family close by? Magnus would have guards such as these, and many more.

He strolled up and down the hall, aware of their eyes following him. *Stay close,* Adrian had said. Blood for the ill was always a tricky thing; too little and all the recipient would feel was languor; too much and they would become frenetic. If Lorenzo took it badly, they would have to make a very rapid exit.

He glanced down at the courtyard below—and then his stomach clenched anew. The card-playing youth was talking to the dark-skinned monk, Domenico, gesturing wildly and pointing at the windows. Only then did the resemblance strike Magnus: that drunken imperiousness, the jaw. This was a son of Lorenzo's, perhaps the unprepared heir.

Tend to your sphere and I will tend to mine. Lorenzo's son, it seemed, was not as keen on that separation.

Magnus leaned against the window, watching. Another youth lounged within the colonnade; there had been at least four gambling. They both wore swords, but Magnus could manage swords. It was the heavier weapons that made matters tricky, the clubs and the maces that could stun and disorient.

As he watched, he heard a rustling behind him and turned to see yet another olive-skinned young man, a wineglass in one hand, a large sheet of paper and a few black sticks clutched in his other. He flopped down before one of the sculptures in the niches, spread the paper on the floor, and began sketching vigorously.

Despite himself, Magnus drew near. At this late hour, with so much wine flowing, he expected to see some joke picture forming, something bawdy or childish. But the drawing was exquisite. In rough charcoal, the marble nymph seemed to find her reflection on the paper—her reflection, and something more, a kind of life that her stone-self lacked. She seemed about to spring into movement, to run or dance. Her creator, Magnus saw now, was barely a man, all wispy black beard and cheeks still child-plump; he dashed the sketch off as one might write a list, then started a more detailed study of the head. This he took more time with, frowning a little as he shaded the jaw, added an artful curl around the ear that the statue lacked.

And for a moment, Magnus forgot it all, forgot Adrian and the book and Lorenzo and their scheming monk, so lost was he in watching that hand move smoothly over the paper. Each stroke exquisitely sensual. The young man glanced over his shoulder, saw Magnus, and gave him a friendly nod before turning back to his paper; without pause, he moved straight to another bare patch and began modeling the nymph's delicate hand.

Miraculous. There was no other word for it—and then Magnus remembered what Fra Girolamo had said. *People starve in the street while you sit here in your palace.* But was this not another form of sustenance, food for a man's spirit? Didn't these studies, at once dashed off and utterly magnificent, did they not also have value? What then of the frescoes, the statues, the very carvings in the wood? Was it all worthless compared to food?

"Magnus," Adrian said softly.

He jumped, feeling almost guilty. The young man looked around again, then took a sip of his wine and continued sketching.

Adrian padded over to him, smoothing down his robe, his tension seemingly dissipated. Magnus glanced at the closed bedroom door. "And?"

"He sleeps," Adrian said.

"The book?"

He didn't reply, only laid a hand on his sternum; Magnus heard a faint crinkling and stared at him. "You took it," he whispered.

Adrian nodded. "I've tied it as tightly as I can, but mind how you touch me," he whispered back.

"What of *I trust in my second?*" He felt suddenly tired, tired in his bones.

"I meant it, Magnus; I still do." Adrian stepped close, lowering his voice until it was nearly inaudible. "But that was before we knew there were copies. You heard the lie as clearly as I did. Even this one is probably a copy."

"How can you tell?"

"You've seen Denèter's library. All their lore is on scrolls. Bound pages like this? It has to be a copy, and if Lorenzo is as canny as his reputation, he probably has several more hidden away." He laid a hand on Magnus's arm. "This is not for Gotland. This is for us to study, so we can figure out what he's planning."

His voice trembled slightly at the last. Was he lying? Magnus couldn't be sure. Adrian's fear obscured everything; perhaps it even obscured Adrian from himself. But there would be time to reason it out later. "What now?" he asked.

Adrian exhaled. "Let us leave, at least for the moment. I need to feed, I need to rest, I need time to think. I cannot do any of these things in Florence."

"About that," Magnus said. He started for the stairs; behind him Adrian paused, examining the sketches with a half-smile before catching up.

"Let me guess," Adrian said as they descended. "Our monk has returned?"

"I'm not sure he left. The other one, Domenico? He's downstairs conferring with the card-players, one of whom resembles Lorenzo il Magnifico." Magnus began rolling up his sleeves, but Adrian shook his head.

"No, Magnus. Let's not make this worse. Give the heir a smacking and Lorenzo may send men after us. We have enough headaches."

"I can see why he's loath to pass the reins—" But he broke off as five young men stepped up to the bottom of the stairs, each with a sword drawn.

"Well, well." In Piero de' Medici's face, Lorenzo's thick features had been softened into something remarkably handsome, if more than a little pouty. "Here they are, my friends: two men in habits, come to rob us."

"Two followers of Fra Girolamo, who are now departing," Adrian corrected. He held up a hand and Magnus stayed his own. A quick glance told him the courtyard had been cleared, though he could smell the guards somewhere nearby.

"Fra Girolamo says otherwise," Piero said.

"I think we should look under their robes," one of his fellows whispered loudly.

"You're welcome to try." Adrian took a step down, and another, Magnus close behind him.

"I am warning you." Piero held out his sword. "You shall not leave until I have checked your person."

Magnus smiled a little. Were all men so alike at this age? All puffed cheeks and bravado. He moved in front of Adrian, envisioning himself larger as he descended the last steps, willing himself vast and menacing and the young men's eyes widening in turn. Even his shadow, he knew, would seem to grow up the walls, becoming gigantic in the courtyard.

"In every man's life, there comes a time when fate speaks to him directly." He reached the ground at last, his chest a hand's breadth from Piero's wavering sword-tip. "You are being spoken to, Piero. Let us pass."

As he spoke, he seized the blade in his hand. They gasped audibly as he slid his hand up to the tip, then held his bloody palm out before them, letting the torchlight play over the raw wound.

He felt the flesh knit even as the air touched it, saw how they crossed themselves, heard their racing hearts and panting gasps. One of the young men's eyes rolled up completely and he dropped in a faint, his sword clattering beside him.

"This is a sign, Piero de' Medici," Magnus said. He coiled and uncoiled his fingers, flexing his smooth, bloodstained palm. "Now we would like to leave, and never return in your lifetime. What will you do?"

To his credit, Piero met Magnus's gaze; and then slowly, carefully, he took a step back, creating just enough space to let them pass. Magnus lowered his hand and began walking, pacing himself to ensure Adrian was close behind him. Ahead, the doors were barred; as they drew close, two men hurried forward to open them, revealing the moonlit street beyond—

There was a scuffling sound behind them, followed by a cry of "don't!" from Piero and an agonizing scream. Magnus whirled about just as Adrian swung one of Piero's friends down by his now-dislocated arm, following with a single swift blow to the throat that cut the scream off. The sword still clutched in his hand was stained with red-black blood, and a gash had been sliced through both the cloak and tunic of Adrian's habit, just above his knees. Piero must have tried to restrain his friend, twisting his lunge into a swipe at Adrian's thighs and oh! had it been any blow but *that*. The youths stumbled back with cries of horror, crossing themselves again, and Magnus knew Adrian's fangs were visible.

"Adrian," he barked.

Adrian rose slowly, his body uncoiling, limbs rippling in the torchlight; he raised his fist to his mouth and licked the blood off his knuckles, his head swaying as he regarded the youths, the guards, all watching him with naked fear on their faces.

"Adrian, *now*."

But Adrian did not respond. Instead he inhaled, a long, low hiss of air, like a man about to burst forth into glorious song, and Magnus felt his stomach drop. To slaughter everyone here, now—

"Steji!" he yelled.

The effect of the word was profound: Adrian whirled about, cringing, eyes wide like a startled doe. Even Magnus felt sick from uttering it. That barked *stop*, what they had dreaded hearing the night they were freed at last. But it brought Adrian out of his haze —and the guards took the opportunity to rush forward, halberds pointed before them. Magnus caught Adrian around the waist, swinging him bodily toward the open doors. They tumbled into the street—

And into a half-circle of monks and men, holding torches and weapons, so many weapons: swords and clubs and pikes and even a few shovels, all at the ready. In their center stood Fra Girolamo, and for once, the monk was smiling.

5

"CREATURES OF HELL!" Fra Girolamo called, his voice ringing over the crowd. "You are in God's sphere now. In the name of the Father, the Son, and the Holy Spirit, begone from this city!"

From behind them, Piero cried, "They have stolen from us! They attacked my father!"

"Shit," Adrian said.

"In the name of Jesus Christ I command you!" Fra Girolamo's voice echoed between the buildings. "Go back to hell where you came from!"

Magnus readied himself as the men rushed at them. Four centuries erin, and still these first moments terrified him. The swords flashing with torchlight as he dodged and punched low, bringing his elbow into another as his fist buried into flesh and bone. No holding back now. The fear in their eyes. He kicked a man and sent him flying backward; a body fell against him, the head twisted halfway round by Adrian's slap. Ducking a halberd to take the man's knees and he caught up a dropped sword and it was like scything wheat then, not bothering to avoid the glancing cuts as he sliced right and left with great sweeps of his arm, blood sluicing the stones beneath his feet, blood sticking his habit to his body. Fra Girolamo's face pale now but his lips still moving. Magnus lunged into a knot of men, feeling blades graze him as he pummeled and stabbed, and when the last one dropped, he saw men on horseback gathering at the end of the street; to a one, they raised crossbows.

"Up," he yelled at Adrian, just as the latter casually rolled a man over his shoulder while keeping a hand protectively over the book.

A man ran at Magnus then, clutching both sword and axe. As large as Magnus, all scars, his eyes black. Swinging and jabbing. Magnus feinted once, twice, keeping out of reach until the man opened his stance; he seized the man by his tunic and yanked him close and bit him in the neck. The surprised cry garbled as Magnus tore away a piece of flesh. The first cascade of crossbow bolts thudded into the man's back like a meaty shield, and then Magnus dropped the body and ran for the palazzo wall, kicking off his sandals and leaping into the air to seize the top of the first window and begin climbing. Adrian already halfway up. Scuttling like spiders. A shower of projectiles rattled around them as the crossbows fired again; Magnus felt a bolt thud into his shoulder, and ignored the pain and kept moving. Above him he saw a bolt bounce off of Adrian's head while another grazed his calf; his cold, dark blood fell onto Magnus's upturned face.

The roof overhung the walls of the palazzo. There was a moment where they were each dangling in the cool night air, legs hanging loose while projectiles sailed just below their feet, and then they swung themselves over the lip and onto the tiles. Without speaking, they tore off their hoods and cloaks; Magnus wrenched the bolt out of his shoulder. Over the roof's edge they glimpsed men crowding at the palazzo door, shouting and pointing up. Torches waved wildly as they milled about, craning their necks to see their quarry.

Magnus peered around in the darkness, then pointed with the bloody bolt. "There's the river. Better odds than the wall."

"But the book—"

Adrian's words were cut off as a bell began tolling, followed by another, and another. Was all of Florence taking up arms against them? Magnus shook his head. "The horsemen will catch us in the fields if we try for the wall. It has to be the river."

Still Adrian hesitated, indecision playing over his features. An arrow hissed between them, its fletching brushing Magnus's face, and bounced off the tiles and down to the street below. They turned to see bodies crowding in the little tower in the center of the roof: a man took aim with a bow while his fellow slung himself carefully onto the tiles, a large knife in each hand. From the courtyard came shouts, mirroring the voices in the street; footsteps thundered beneath the roof, as of many bodies ascending.

The bow fired again. Adrian snatched the arrow mid-flight with a frustrated cry and lunged forward, taking three running steps to seize the knife-wielder and fling him into the night air like he were nothing more than paper. The screams of terror from below echoed the screaming in the tower as the men tried to retreat, but Adrian was already there, his fists flashing up and down as he punched and punched. When at last he stepped back, his arms were glistening to his elbows, his white sleeves dripping with blood.

"There has to be another way," he said, as if there had been no interruption.

Magnus looked down at the street again, at the splattered corpse and the panicked crowd. "River," he snapped. "You can do as you please."

He began running across the roof, not looking back—he refused to look back—but he didn't run quite as fast as he could, and just as he reached the edge, he heard Adrian behind him. They leapt across a street, then down and up and down again as they ran from roof to roof, their bare feet slapping the terra cotta as regular as drumbeats. As they leapt across an alley, a shout went up, a cry that seemed to repeat itself from street to street, all the way back to the mob, which was flowing after them. Still Magnus and Adrian ran, heading for the black ribbon of the Arno and its swift current, the moonlight dancing invitingly on its surface.

To their left the cathedral loomed massive and silent, its dome blotting out the stars, casting the world below into darkness. More tomb than church now. A triumph of humanity—but Magnus's humanity was a long time ago, never to return. He had a sudden vision of a coiling serpent as vast as the dome and nearly fell, tumbling a story's height from one roof to the next while behind him Adrian leapt as graceful as a deer. Later, later. If there was to be a later.

An arrow clattered behind them, and another; hoofbeats clattered in the street below. "Look for a boat," Adrian called, and Magnus nearly swore at him but bit it back, instead pushing himself faster. The river lay straight ahead, a gully between the buildings on either side. Behind them a man called out; Magnus glanced back to see a party of figures climbing up from a balcony, where an archer balanced and took aim. Adrian's cursing loud in the night as the first arrow sailed over their heads. They were nearly there—

Magnus reached the edge of the last roof and flung himself into the air, realizing too late that there was a promenade between the buildings and the river and he wasn't going to clear it—

Instead, he fell in a roll on the paved surface and looked up to see a dozen horsemen with crossbows, all aimed at him.

Magnus bared his fangs and roared, a bellowing cry that made everyone recoil. A few shot their bolts but they flew wildly, grazing his arm and leg, one slicing through the skirt of his tunic. He lunged like a bull first one way and then another, making the horses rear and plunge, shoving feet out of stirrups and smacking crossbows aside, thinking *act large* thinking *act rabid*. Blades sliced the air as the men shouted and cursed, struggling to steady their mounts, who were wisely trying to flee. No heaven for horses. He pulled a rider off just as the fellow reloaded, swinging the crossbow about and firing at the others, pulling the arm from its socket without thinking as he used the body as a shield. The horse fleeing and the others trying desperately to follow. Mist swirled about them, and through the rearing horses, he saw Adrian drop neatly onto the promenade and, without stopping, vault onto the back of a horse and break the rider's neck. He shoved the corpse off and tried to get the horse under control, holding out his hand to Magnus while the animal reared and bucked.

An explosion cut across the melee, and white heat shot past Magnus's face to strike Adrian's horse. They tumbled atop him, horse and Adrian alike, the horse shrieking in pain. His mind conjured up a single word *arquebus* and then all was limbs and bodies and falling, they were falling into the river, men and horses were falling with them and everywhere were screams and he struck a piling and bounced into the water. The cold, rushing water like a slap. A man landed atop him; Magnus shoved him off and kicked himself deeper into the water and was at once aware of the bolts in his flesh still, of myriad cuts healing. He blew out the air from his lungs and let himself sink, let himself be carried along as he twisted and tugged at the shafts, ripping them out one by one, tearing muscle and skin, and the water stinging. Only when his lungs were aching did he cautiously break the surface. He was drifting beneath a bridge flanked by anchored barges; behind him, there was a fire-bright glow on the promenade where a crowd had formed, throwing ropes to the men and their horses struggling against the current. A few desultory arrows sailed harmlessly into the river.

Closer to the city walls came the smell of tanneries, and then the river slid gently past the towers into the open countryside. At last he saw Adrian climbing onto a bank and began stroking toward him. As he dragged himself out of the water, his ankle shrieked in pain from a broken bolt still embedded deep. Adrian held out his hand and Magnus seized it, let himself be pulled onto the grassy riverbank where he just sat, exhausted, before turning to his ankle. His bare arms, he saw now, were laced with healing cuts from the evening's blades; his tunic was in tatters, his papers a sodden lump against his chest. He felt tired and foolish and angry: at Adrian, at Gabriel, at the monk, at the sheer waste of it all.

Adrian dragged up the hem of his tunic and tore off the sodden binding around his chest, prying the book free. He tried to fan it open but the pages clumped together. "I think it can still be salvaged," he said. "If we can get it to a bookbinder, they might—"

With a grunt, Magnus levered himself up and stumbled over to Adrian. He jerked the book from Adrian's hands, flung it into the river, and sat back down hard on the muddy grass, where he once more set to working the bolt free.

There was silence from above, and then, querulous: "What did you just do?"

Magnus rocked the shaft one way and another, whining with pain; with a last gasp, he pulled it free and flung it after the book.

"Magnus, we have to know exactly what that book says," Adrian continued, his voice shaking now. "Gabriel wants it for a reason. If we don't know what his purpose is, we'll be blindsided again—"

"I won't keep doing this," Magnus said.

Adrian fell silent, looking at him hollowly. His hand had dropped to the back of his thigh, where it was rubbing his skin through the gash in his tunic. Magnus knew what he was trying to rub away, that somewhere inside him was still a terrified, hamstrung boy, just as Magnus carried a terrified, dying young man within himself. Perhaps all of Gabriel's erines had something similar.

"You need to choose, Adrian. Either you give yourself over to currying Gabriel's favor, in which case we will part ways here and now, or you set yourself to steering clear of him. You cannot do both. You will tear yourself in two, all while helping him to even greater power, perhaps world-destroying power. That book"—he gestured at the river—"is at the very least an excuse to overthrow Denèter, and if there is some form of pure blood out there? It doesn't matter whether this Great Return happens in three days or three centuries. We cannot let ourselves get caught up in his plotting. *We won't make it.*"

The wind gusted over them, twisting Adrian's wet tunic against his body and plastering his hair to his face, making him look more a boy than ever. For so long, Magnus had only seen him as a force to be obeyed, one to whom he was abjectly grateful for this second life, however small and ugly. Now, however, he was imagining what Adrian must have been like before Gabriel took him, and the vision made Magnus's heart hurt.

"You would leave me?" Adrian whispered.

No, he nearly said. *No, no, I will never leave you.* Anything to take away that frightened expression, so much worse than the worst rages. Instead, he made himself speak calmly. "If the choice is between leaving and watching him twist you into another Seissan, or even a Thaddeus? Yes. I cannot, I *will not* be party to that." And clamped his lips down before he said anything more, before he could talk himself into amendments and apologies.

He thought there might be tears then, even hysterics, and how would he keep from yielding? But Adrian just stared at him, his eyes shimmering in the moonlight, his lips slightly parted.

Finally, Adrian murmured something inaudible; he cleared his throat and said more loudly, "Agreed."

Magnus frowned at him. "'Agreed, I'm off to Gotland,' or—"

"Agreed, we steer clear of him." But his voice trembled at the words, and the first tears began spilling over his cheeks. "It's just—if we anger him again, Magnus? You're right: I won't make it. I don't think I can take it again. I thought I was stronger ... but it was so much worse this time, and I, I—"

Magnus got to his feet and held him.

THEY PLODDED along a wide road churned lumpish from cart wheels, flanked by open hills dotted with scrubby trees, watching the softly undulating horizon for the first hints of purple. An arm's width of space between them. They had dodged something terrible, Magnus knew; dodged it but not banished it.

"Do you remember the night I made you erin?" Adrian asked.

His whole body suddenly nerveless. They had dodged something terrible, only to have Adrian's mind turn to this? He tried to think of a distraction, something witty; he could think of nothing. "Yes," he said.

"You've never asked me why I did it." Now Adrian was looking at him, his expression unreadable. "Have you ever wanted to?"

Again Magnus tried to think of something to change the subject; again he came up with nothing. "Sometimes," he said. Which had the benefit of being both true and succinct. Another lesson he had learned in Gotland: the briefer the answer, the better the outcome.

"But you were afraid of what I would say?"

"Yes." Before Adrian could continue, he said quickly, "Do you really want to talk about this now?"

Even as he spoke, however, the memories were starting to return. The shock of that night, hired mercenaries protecting a speck of a village. The panic so overwhelming, he hadn't even felt the wound, hadn't realized he'd been struck until he fell on the sand halfway to the boats and felt the viscera sliding from his open stomach. His fellows racing past him, over him, stepping on him as if he were already dead—

"I want you to know why." Adrian's voice was maddeningly calm. "I made you erin because I wanted to know what Gabriel felt when he hurt me. I wanted to *be* Gabriel; I wanted to do to someone else what he did to me. I am not proud of it," he pressed before Magnus could speak. "I am anything but proud of it. The things I asked of you, forced you to—" He broke off. "I just—I wanted you to know that I am sorry for it, truly sorry."

Magnus looked at him, waiting to see if there was more—and then he exhaled. "For fuck's sake," he said. "I knew *that*." At Adrian's visible surprise, he found himself smiling. "It was a long time ago, Adrian."

"But you just said—"

"What I've never known is why you chose *me*. That raid was a slaughter; you had your pick of dying oafs. I just never knew if it was sheer chance, or if there was some calculation—and if you ever regretted it," he added in a smaller voice.

"Oh." Adrian fell silent, his brow furrowing. A bat fluttered lazily overhead, and Magnus let his eyes follow it, watching its black silhouette against the fading stars. How many nights since that first one? Thousands upon thousands. So strange that they hadn't spoken of it before. Though perhaps this too was Gotland, somehow.

"In all honesty?" he finally said. "I chose you because you were still crawling. All the others, they were praying, weeping, waiting to die. You had been gutted like a fish and you were still trying to crawl—" He broke off, then touched Magnus's arm. "I'm sorry. I didn't mean to remind you of it."

His fellows fleeing. No one even glancing down while he cried and pleaded. Hearing rather than seeing the ships being shoved into the water, knowing he was being abandoned. His body numbing while his mind beat against his skull in raw panic. The icy, rising tide sucking at him and in the distance the thwacking of cudgels against bone as the mercenaries staved in the skulls of the dying. More terrified than he had ever been before or since and his heart beating so fast he thought it would burst—

And then he had looked up and seen that slim shadow, fangs glistening in the moonlight and hands reaching for him, and his mouth had formed the word *yes* even though he had no breath left for it.

"It was a long time ago," he repeated.

"But our pasts are always present." Adrian paused. "What I meant to say is that I chose you because even knowing you could not survive, you still fought to live. At the time, I told myself you would … endure more." He swallowed audibly. "Later, though, I realized I chose you because I was too frightened to either live or die, and somehow I thought you might give me strength. And you have, Magnus, again and again, even when I would much rather wallow in my cowardice." He fell silent again, then laughed, a short exhale. "Do you know, there have been times when I've stayed alive just to spite you—but as you would say, there are worse reasons."

Magnus, who had been about to say just that, only smiled.

"And I have *never* regretted it. Not once, not even in Gotland. What you said in the library—" Adrian took a breath. "I don't ever want to hear you say that again, Magnus. Don't say it, don't even think it. Swear to me that you won't."

He swallowed, forcing down the sudden lump in his throat. "I swear," he said hoarsely.

The dark head looked away. "I didn't think you would stay if you knew why I had made you," he said to the fields.

"We were both different then," Magnus said. "By the time I became someone who would leave, you had become a better man, so it was moot."

"As simple as that?"

"Does it need to be more complicated?"

For a moment there was only the sound of their bare feet padding on the hard earth. Then, soft: "Perhaps not." Before Magnus could reply, he continued in a firmer voice, "You do realize I'm going to be all nerves for the next fifty years at least, seeing the Skìa everywhere, thinking every letter a demand for our return."

Magnus snorted. "As opposed to the last fifty years, when you were a paragon of reason and calm?"

"Asshole." But Adrian was smiling as he said it, a real smile.

And Magnus had many more half-formed thoughts: about how every night was another chance for something better, about when to simply live and when to take a stand—but they had dodged something terrible, had perhaps even come out the better for it, and good gamblers knew when to take their winnings.

Instead, he moved closer to Adrian and gave him a nudge. "So, these nerves of yours. Will they permit us to seek shelter, or should I expect fifty years of digging holes to sleep in?"

"I am not sleeping in dirt and neither are you," Adrian said. "We have suffered too many indignities tonight as it is."

"Shelter it is, then," he replied, yawning as he craned his neck around. "I don't see any buildings, maybe we should cut across the fields—"

"Too many indignities," Adrian continued, "and it seems the night is not done with us yet."

Magnus blinked, then peered ahead at Adrian's nod; his good humor fell away.

There were three horses on a little rise close to the road, their riders standing nearby in conference. Two figures all in black, from their hose to their doublets to the cloaks they wore over all, while their third was a small, stocky man in a green velvet jerkin and wine-colored hose, his balding head ringed by black bristles. As they caught sight of Magnus and Adrian, he stepped forward, his arms at his sides, his upper body stiff. Like a puppet, Magnus thought, his eyes flashing from Seissan to the two Skìa behind him. A puppet and the shadows of their master.

"What did I just say about my nerves," Adrian muttered.

"Let's hope your Lorenzo hid his copies well," Magnus said.

"Oh, he's my Lorenzo now, is he?" But Adrian's expression was somber.

As they drew close, Seissan raised his chin, which brought him level with Magnus's chest. "Adrian," he said. "And the pet block-head. Do you have it?"

"Seissan." Adrian spread his arms with a wry smile. Their tattered habits were still damp and mud-splattered, while Seissan looked as if he had just left court. "Does it look like we have it?"

"Then the task remains unfinished." A smile touched Seissan's thin lips and just as quickly vanished. "Am I right in supposing I would do well to let the waters still in Florence before I make my own attempt?"

"Oh, we would not want to delay you," Magnus said. "I'm sure they'll welcome you with open arms."

"Meaning you made a mess of it as usual," Seissan retorted. "If another dangen finds out—"

"I'm not sure it will matter," Adrian cut in. His voice cool now, his posture straight. "A word of advice, Seissan: I would not bring him that book."

"Pardon?" The smaller man blinked, not once but several times. *Puppet*, Magnus thought again.

"I am loyal, but I'm not foolish," Adrian continued in the same cool tone. "Something else is at work in this. He may be culling again, or he may have caught wind of a plot against him. You know how he feels about betrayal."

"As do you, better than most," Seissan snapped. At his raised voice, the Skìa moved forward; impatiently, he waved them back. "I have no idea what you're talking about, Adrian, nor do I want to know. I do not ask questions. I do my duty. I do my duty because I don't want to end up like *you*."

Adrian merely shrugged. "As you wish. It was a friendly warning, nothing more."

Seissan blinked again; and then he burst out laughing. The sound, high-pitched and screeching, made Magnus's hackles rise. Instinctively, he stepped closer to Adrian, while behind Seissan the two Skìa moved their hands beneath their cloaks. "A friendly warning, eh?" He dabbed his eyes. "Oh tell me more, Your Highness. Gabriel's favorite toy, doling out friendly warnings. But that's not the truth of it, is it? The truth of it is you fucked up *again*. The truth of it is you want to frighten me into running off so you can try again, and again, until you and your idiot get it right."

Through the tirade Magnus was watching the Skìa and Seissan both, readying himself. Seissan was of Gabriel's blood and a century honed, but the two Skìa were young and wet-mouthed, their bellies visibly curving. Foolish, to drink so heavily beyond the safety of Gotland, but it made the odds considerably better.

"You would have *me* obey *you* and go back to Gabriel empty-handed." Seissan was spitting the words now. "Oh, it is nothing for you; he adores his lovely lovely boy, his precious prize. But it is *everything* to me." He lunged forward, inches from Adrian, his watery eyes slitted. "It is everything to me, Adrian. So, take your friendly warning and shove it up your ass, if you can fit it around his cock."

Magnus stepped forward smoothly, placing himself between them. He kept his hands low and wide and simply stood there, looking down at Seissan with as neutral an expression as he could manage. As tense as a bowstring. Gemma, Vincent, they could be cruel, but it was always a calculated cruelty. Seissan, however, had snapped more than once in his time, with terrifying results.

"It's all right, Magnus," Adrian said from behind him. "We said our piece, and the sun is nearly up." He bowed. "I hope you get what you deserve, Seissan."

He touched Magnus's arm, and he too bowed; they began heading back to the road.

"Adrian," Seissan called.

Adrian glanced at Magnus, and then he turned around.

"Did you actually see the book?" He gestured to the Skìa; one placed a pair of riding gloves in his hand while the other draped a cloak over his shoulders.

"I did," Adrian said.

"What is it?"

Adrian nodded at the Skìa, and with a sigh, Seissan pointed them back to the horses. They waited in silence, the seconds stretching out, until the Skìa were out of earshot and their backs were turned. Only then did Adrian mouth *Taiart Gal*.

Seissan's eyebrows arched. "*Really?* Well, well." He drew on his gloves and punched his fingers together, a smile curling his mouth. "Now, that *is* interesting. Still with Lorenzo, I presume?"

"You'll have to ask him," Adrian said.

"Well, well," he said again. He tied his cloak, then smoothed down the bristles of his hair. "All very interesting; it almost makes me believe you. You'll understand, of course, that I would see this for myself."

"Your thoroughness is admirable as always, Seissan," Adrian drawled. He started to turn away, then paused, as if suddenly struck by a thought. "It was the strangest thing; the book came to the Medici as surety for a loan. Curious, wouldn't you say?"

"Oh, very curious, and precisely the kind of detail to give credence to your claim," Seissan retorted. "Gabriel is dangling the book to see what we'll do; is that what you think? But you are undone by your own story, Adrian. If the book is what you say, Gabriel would never have let it go." He gave a bark of laughter. "He would sell *you* long before he would yield such a treasure."

"As you say," Adrian said with a shrug.

"Indeed. And if you had listened to what I said when you last visited Gotland, matters might have been less *distressing*. But you won't make that mistake again, will you?"

"No." Adrian looked at Magnus. "No, we won't make that mistake again."

Magnus smiled at him then, and Adrian smiled back.

"There's an inn down the road," Seissan said with a dismissive jerk of his head. "Flea-ridden, but the serving wench had nice tits. Though they may send you straight to the stables in those ... garments."

"Or they may simply attack us, since your lads have already entertained themselves?" Adrian gestured to the Skìa.

"I'm not that foolish," Seissan snapped. "We were held up on the road here; there's pieces of bandit spread across three fields. You should be fine for a day." He glanced at the Skìa, shaking his head. "Spoilt, the lot of them. All wet mouths and swollen veins. Not like we were, eh?"

"We never had the luxury," Adrian replied. "You could always spare us the price of a day's lodging, as fellow servants of our king."

At that, Seissan smiled. "Adrian! I'm surprised you would even ask. Why, you've already raised the alarm in Florence. Two strangers in filthy habits, yet with a fistful of good coin? It's an invitation to suspicion." He let his eyes roam down to their feet and back again. "Far safer to remain just as you are."

The Skìa rode up, leading Seissan's horse. He swung himself nimbly into the saddle and looked down at them, still smiling. "I thank you for locating the book," he said, "even if you've made it harder to get."

"If you bring it to him, you have greater balls than I do."

"Oh, I have balls, all right," Seissan agreed. "Oh, and Adrian?" He paused for a beat, holding Adrian's gaze. "I want very much to tell him you helped me in this; God knows you could use the testimonial. But you know how he easily he detects falsehood …" He looked sorrowfully at the heavens, then suddenly held up a finger. "Of course, if I felt certain you would aid me in the future, *then* I could praise you with the full weight of truth."

Adrian said nothing, just met his gaze evenly; but it seemed to be enough. He grinned and leaned down from his horse. "Our little secret," he said, slapping Adrian hard on the shoulder before urging his horse into a fast trot, the Skìa falling in behind him.

Magnus watched them leave, shaking his head. "I have a bad feeling about that."

"I have a terrible feeling about that," Adrian said as he turned and began plodding up the road once more. "But as you said, Magnus: someone will bring Gabriel that book, even if they have to invent it from whole cloth. Better Seissan than many." At Magnus's astonishment he rolled his eyes. "Yes, I heard you that night, and yes, you were right yet again." He waved his hand dismissively. "Anyway. Let us hope he was telling the truth about this inn; perhaps they'll let us sleep in the stable."

Magnus, still taken aback, shook himself at that. "Perhaps I can spare us one more indignity." He pulled up the hem of his tunic and began working out the coins. "I don't know what the world is coming to, when two novices can be assaulted on the road, but at least I had the presence of mind to keep our money safe."

Adrian watched the coins drop out of the cloth, his eyes shining. "Magnus! You are brilliant. Truly the best erin I ever created."

"I'm the only erin you ever created."

"Because I knew no other would come close," Adrian replied promptly.

For a few minutes they walked in companionable silence, watching the purpling sky overtaking the stars. Then, soft: "Magnus?"

He looked attentively at Adrian.

"Lorenzo confessed that he had astronomers inspect the book. There is mention of a comet, with a specific trajectory … it won't be soon. But the map of the heavens is plausible. I cannot imagine a giant snake falling from the sky, and yet …" He dug his fingernails into his palm, watching as the skin split and bled and closed again.

Magnus only shrugged. "Well, if it's not to be soon, then we have plenty of time to arrange more pleasant deaths for ourselves. Though I don't think Gabriel will wait to antagonize the others."

"No, he's been chomping at the bit to challenge Denèter once and for all," Adrian said moodily. "We may not have much time for anything."

"Is that an invitation to wager?"

"What?" He stared at Magnus, aghast. "Certainly not!"

"We don't have to use money," Magnus tapped his lip. "We could each bet a new shirt, for example. In a nice, soft linen."

"Oh, now I see why you were in such a sulk."

"I never sulk. You, on the other hand—"

"Magnus." Adrian smiled at him tiredly. "I will buy you another shirt."

Magnus draped his arm around his shoulders. "I accept your apology," he said. "Do you know where they have excellent tailors?"

As Adrian leaned against him, he smiled down at the dark head. "Barcelona."

"A little chaotic there, no?" Adrian yawned.

"All the better to disappear for a while."

"And what excuse do we have for going to Barcelona?"

"I'm sure we'll think of something by the time we get there."

Adrian laughed, but he pressed closer to Magnus. "If the prophecy is true—"

"Adrian." He held out his own hand before them, turning his filthy yet unmarked palm one way and another. "Just as our existence lends truth to that tale? So we are proof that anything is possible, good and bad. Who knows? Maybe the serpent will indeed come, and do us all a favor by landing right on Gabriel's head."

They rounded a bend in the road, circling a copse of gnarled olive trees, and it was then that they saw it: the dark humps of the first farmhouses, the denser mass of a village beyond. Like sighting land after weeks at sea; it made something unknot deep in Magnus's belly.

"Magnus," Adrian murmured from beneath his arm. "If you would rather have the room to yourself ..."

"What?" He looked down at the bowed head, alarmed. "Why would you ask that?" When there was no response, he slowed their pace, ducking his head to catch Adrian's eye. "Adrian, if I ever don't want to share your bed, I will say so, never fear. And none of this business of the past being present," he pressed as Adrian started to speak. "I am *choosing* to share a bed with you. As long as you don't kick me," he added quickly. "If you kick me, I may just send you to the stable."

"As simple as that?" But Adrian was starting to smile again.

"It's as simple as we choose to make it."

"I'm glad you're here, Magnus."

His whole body warming at the words, as warm as that first night he had awakened and found himself whole once more, all the pain and cold banished. A second chance. What was all they had suffered since, compared to that singular gift?

"As am I." He brushed his lips against Adrian's head. "Now please, would you pick up your pace, unless you want to explain our blisters to the innkeeper?"

Adrian yawned but complied. Arms draped around each other, they passed the first tended fields, heard the distant bleating of sheep being guided out for the day. The horizon tinged red as the village became distinct against the backdrop of gently rolling hills; trails of smoke rose from the thatched roofs into the lightening sky. Adrian's cool, living body under his arm and the taste of dew in the air. What would he not endure again for this? Lorenzo had asked what they valued, and here was an answer Magnus could honestly give: the feel of another's skin, the taste of dew, the endless wager that each new night might bring hope as well as fear, healing as well as hurt. Every night another chance. He would never not be grateful for it.

ABOUT THE SERIES

If you enjoyed this book, dear reader, there will be more. *Seeds of Truer Natures* is a prequel to my novel series Prima Materia. The first book in the series will be published in 2022, or you can join the read-along at primamateria.online, where I'll be serializing each novel in parts prior to their publication. You'll also get access to deleted scenes, research notes, and more—and your subscription will help fund the writing and production of these books. Learn more at primamateria.online.

GLOSSARY

cagè: captain.

cifet: advisor. The second who whispers in the ear of their master.

dangen, dangenes: family or house; that is, all the descendants of a particular sereides. There are nine dangenes in the world. The Berger are one of the five dangenes currently in Europe.

erin, erines: a human whose physiology had been altered by a transfusion of sereides' or erin's blood; what will later become known as a vampyr or vampire.

genetes: sire. The one whose blood is drunk by the human so as to enact the transformation.

Nagac: the mythical serpent that descended from the sky two millennia ago, whose blood transformed the first nine into the Sereideas.

Sereidenikè: the language of the sereidees. A thickly-syllabled tongue that evolves but slowly, much like its speakers.

sereides, sereidees: those who believe they carry the serpent's blood in their veins. Sereidees possess unnatural degrees of longevity, strength, and subsist primarily on human blood consumed by piercing veins with long, retractable fangs. Many have patches of scales covering their spines, torsos, and faces, and brilles to protect their eyes.

Skìa: shadow. Also the name of the chosen agents of Gabriel Berger, both sereidees and erines, who dress all in black and enact his will throughout Europe. Depending on who you ask, their costume is either carefully calculated to intimidate, or because the Skìa are ponces who rely on show rather than skill, or both.

steji: stop! A command, usually uttered in terrible circumstances.

Taiart Gal: the Great Return. The foretold return of the Nagac, though why it would bother coming back remains a mystery.

A Pronunciation Guide

Most of the letters are pronounced as in English, with a few exceptions:

> *a, e,* and *i* are pronounced as in Spanish or Italian
> *c* is pronounced *sh*
> *g* is pronounced as a hard *g*, as in *give*
> *j* is pronounced as a soft *g*, as in *general*

Unless indicated by an accent `, the first syllable is stressed.

ACKNOWLEDGMENTS

Seeds of Truer Natures was inspired by a wonderful talk Ada Palmer gave at FOGcon 8 on the topic of Florence and censorship. Listening to Dr. Palmer reminded me of all that I love about scholarship, and opened up to me a whole period of history with which I only had passing familiarity. When I was drafting this book, in the first months of COVID-19 lockdown, I dared to email Dr. Palmer with further questions, and she responded far more generously than this little project deserved. This book would not exist without her.

They say writing is a solitary task, but no story of mine has ever been the product of just myself. I'm indebted to my fellow authors E.C. Ambrose, Kate Heartfield, E.M. Markoff, Christi Nogle, and Catherine Schaff-Stump for their critiques. Valentina Zucchi shared with me both historical insights and floor plans for the Palazzo Medici, which has been expanded and renovated since the time of this story. Kat Howard gave, as always, a wonderful developmental edit, and Jon Reyes provided nuanced editorial feedback on the final draft. For some years now, I've worked with Dr. Olivier Simon to create and develop Sereidenikè, and it was as always a joy to further shape the lexicon. Richard Shealy took on the daunting task of corralling my prose into something resembling English grammar, and Najla Qamber designed the cover using Welder Wings' artwork. This story bears all their fingerprints, and I am deeply grateful for their contributions.

ABOUT THE AUTHOR

L.S. Johnson was born in New York and now lives in Northern California, where she feeds her cats by writing book indices. She is the author of over forty short stories and the Chase and Daniels series of gothic novellas, including *Harkworth Hall, Leviathan, The Painter's Widow*, and the forthcoming *A Shining Path*. Her first collection, *Vacui Magia*, won the North Street Book Prize and was a finalist for the World Fantasy Award. Her second collection, *Rare Birds*, is now available. She is currently working on Prima Materia, a historical fantasy series set in Enlightenment-era Europe. Find her online and sign up for her newsletter at www.traversingz.com.

CPSIA information can be obtained
at www.ICGtesting.com
Printed in the USA
FSHW012259171121
86228FS

9 780998 893693